Eternal Vow

by

Julie A. D'Arcy

Cover Art by *Teddi Black*

The Wild Rose Press, Inc.
PO Box 708
Adams Basin, NY 14410-0708
Visit us at www.thewildrosepress.com

Publishing History
First Edition, 2024
Trade Paperback ISBN 978-1-5092-5711-9
Digital ISBN 978-1-5092-5712-6

Published in the United States of America

Eternal Night

I dwelled in a time long past,
When love a song sweet,
Darkness down inside I weep.
Eternal is the night.

I walk with the dead,
Pray with the living,
That I will find the strength,
To raise my head,
Walk out of the place of the damned,
Find my soul,
Drink my fear,
Raise my face to the light.
Eternal is the night.

By Julie. A. D'Arcy

Dedication

To my beloved parents Dorothy Joan Brauman and James Stephen Borserio—may they both rest in peace—thank you for always being there for me and your words of reassurance.

This is also to thank my talented daughter Tegan for the names Alara and Charlie, and to my daughter Errin, my solace and calming influence, who suggested the idea for the first chapter.

Acknowledgements

This is for all my friends and family who helped me through the most difficult time of my life. Without friends and family, really, who would we be?

Prologue

London, August 1796

A chill ran down the length of Vincent's body as a gust of icy wind penetrated his greatcoat. He dragged his coat more securely about his shoulders and drew the collar up snugly around his neck. It would not do to develop the ague this early in the Season.

The cobblestones glittered black and slippery from the rain. His hair, now damp, hung in a heavy knot down his back. He cursed, wishing he had not dismissed his coachman so readily, but he had not intended to bed Lady Charlotte later that evening. However, the opportunity had presented itself and who was he to deny the lady his company. He gave the night a contented smile.

Over his shoulder horses' hooves skidded on the wet cobblestones, and the jingle of a harness rang excessively loud in the crisp night air as a carriage drew to a halt.

He threw a quick look behind him and noted Lord Wilkes had returned earlier than expected from his club. He smiled into the night and struck up a jaunty whistle, twirling his cane with dexterous ease and continued his stride down the road toward St. James Palace and the Star and Garter Gentleman's club.

However, no more than five paces away he noted a

figure separate from the shadow of a stone wall. His footsteps faltered and his fingers tightened on the head of his cane. "Show yourself. I demand it."

A woman glided from the darkness to await in the glow of an overhead lantern. She threw back her hood as he drew near.

Vincent's eyes widened, but he regained his composure as her voluptuous curves and the scent of her perfume filled his senses.

Artful tendrils of her ebony hair escaped from the coil plaited about her head, appearing like fine strands of silk upon her pale cheeks. A sparkling clip at the throat of her velvet cloak denoted her a lady and a gown of scarlet and gold sported an indecently low neckline. However, it was as if she felt no cold.

The moon broke from the cloud overhead, and Vincent watched mesmerized as several large raindrops trickled down the valley between her breasts. She released not a shiver but remained focused brazenly on his face.

Her dark red lips formed a small bow in her pale face, and Vincent's body quickened, hot and hard, but he drew himself under control. Her eyes told him of her confidence in her beauty and her interest. There would be plenty of time.

He remained silent…enthralled. He realized now this woman was familiar. He had spied on her earlier from his private box at Covent Garden. Their gazes had locked, and she had beckoned to him across the crowded auditorium with her smile alone, but he'd managed to break eye contact when Lady Charlotte touched his arm and spoke quietly into his ear. Sometime later when he had stepped from the theater, he had collided with her. Her turquoise eyes had held him transfixed.

Using all his will, he had broken from her magnetic hold, apologized, and moved out into the night to his carriage. Those same eyes yet again now held him captivated—unusually bright and sparkling in the night.

"Can I help you?" His Italian accent came particularly thick in his state of unrest. He'd had audiences with royalty and not felt so ill at ease.

"I fear I have lost my escort." The woman smiled and curled her red tipped fingers around his arm. "Dreadful man, stunk of garlic and lavender water." She laughed softly and Vincent relaxed, detecting an accent in her voice. "You were no doubt clever in losing him." He laughed in turn. "May I inquire after the gentleman's name?"

"Lord Henry Delmar. Do you know him?"

"Unfortunately, not."

"Unfortunately?" She raised a shapely brow. His words seemed to confuse her.

"Or I might be tempted to challenge him to a duel for leaving such a beautiful woman unattended this dreadful night." He smiled and placed his hand over hers. The coldness of her skin penetrating through his gloves gave him pause. However, her next words distracted him.

"I had intended to catch one of your hackney cabs, but sadly such a vehicle is not to be had." She looked away. "I do not suppose I could bother you for an escort back to my lodgings."

"I, myself was foolhardy enough to dismiss my carriage earlier this evening, but I would be happy to walk you, if you allow it." He scanned the dimly lit street, paying attention to the deep shadows beneath the towering oaks across the road. "London is not known for its hospitality this time of night."

"I have lodgings in Grosvenor Square if it is not inconvenient."

He nodded. "My father owns a townhouse in Grosvenor Square. Fifty-three." He ran a hand through his sodden hair as the rain ran down his face.

"My house is forty-two. We are almost neighbors." She touched a hand to his arm. "Shall we be on our way then?"

He stepped back. "I think firstly, introductions are in order." He swept her a low bow. "Lord Vincent D'Armano, previously from Hampshire." He touched his lips to her fingertips, again noticing the chill of her skin.

"Italian?"

"Venetian." He smiled.

Another soft laugh escaped her lips. "Most enjoyable city, Venice. I had such an…interesting time the last time I visited." She sighed. "The city of lovers."

"Was it?"

She looked at him coyly from beneath her lashes allowing a silence to settle before she spoke again. "I think I shall keep that information to myself." She placed a slim gloved hand on his arm, and he covered it with his.

His eyes met hers. "And what name do I call you, my beauty of the night?"

"You may call me…" She touched a finger to her mouth drawing attention to the redness of her heart-shaped lips. "Epatha. Mmm. Yes, I think that will do nicely." Her perfect white teeth glowed in the night, her face taking on the appearance of fine white porcelain in the moonlight.

He leaned forward to raise her hood over her rain-moistened hair, accidentally stroking the soft curve of her cheek. "Lady Epatha, it will be then," he replied softly. "And is there no last name?"

She lowered her lashes and chuckled softly as she led him forward. "Just Epatha will do, as you must allow a lady some mystery."

Strange, exotic, beautiful, like the woman herself. Vincent laughed softly and they strode on into the darkness. For several streets they walked in silence, passing tightly packed townhouses, small parks, and tall ancient buildings of all stature and status. Finally, Epatha drew to a halt in front of the remains of an abandoned inn. A large, white, half-broken sign hung sideways several feet above them, pronouncing the building *The Last Chancery*. The doors and windows boarded black, yet its pale brick stood out in stark relief against the grimness of the night, painting the building with an Old World charm.

"This is a shortcut," she purred, gliding past him into the dark alley alongside the building. "Follow, I will lead you."

"I don't think—" He reached out to recapture her arm, but she slipped from his grasp into the alley. "How do you know this place?" he called, searching the darker shadows lurking across the road.

"Lord Delmar walked me this way this morning."

Still, he did not follow, something was not quite right. Gingerly, he stepped to the edge of the lane and peered into the black. Well-bred young ladies did not appear out of nowhere to lead gentlemen into dark alleys where cutthroats could be lingering. His fingers tightened on the head of his cane. "My lady, we should keep to the well-lit streets."

"Are you afraid, my handsome escort?" Her lilting voice sounded just inside the alleyway.

"Of course, I am not afraid." He took a step forward. He had won a decent number of boxing matches at his club, and the small poniard imbedded in the head of his sword-cane and freed at the twirl of the handle should see him safe. But it was sheer recklessness to venture into one of these hellholes in the dead of night when there was a safer course to take.

Her voice echoed from within the darkness. "Where is your sense of adventure, my lord? I took you as a man of caliber."

"Madam, I must insist you come out of there at once!"

Then it came, and he had no other choice than to listen. A sound unlike any he had heard before, compelling him in a sweet lingering song from the depths of the darkness. A siren's song—strong, melodious, it hailed from far, yet spoke right into his head, wrapping its silky smooth strands of rich caramel, of promises of soft caresses, warm lips, and a hot melding of flesh around and into his brain.

"Come bring me to life. Come share the dark. My spirit sleeps, my soul is numb, only you can free me. Wake me. Bid my blood to run before I am lost. Come lay with me, you are the one, you are my eternity."

Her voice encircled him, ensnared him, and encompassed him in its deadly siren's call. His body responded to the dark sensual images she provoked and overrode his common sense. He took one step, then two. He was a fool, but he could not resist. The alley held only darkness and the sky above matched the mood, perfect ebony. His skin prickled as he continued to put one foot in front of the other.

A movement to his left had him spinning. "Epatha?" Her name slipped from his lips on a hoarse whisper. "Is that you singing? What are you doing?"

No answer came.

Then the moon broke through the clouds, and he viewed her, leaning against a brick wall. The hood of her cloak fell back from her thick black hair, painting her part of the night, pale, ethereal. Her smile embodied beguilement as she unclipped her cloak, allowing it to drop to the ground. Vincent's temples pounded, and his blood burned.

She held out her arms, and his gentlemanly instincts fled. She was offering, and he had never been one to refuse what a beautiful woman freely offered. He strode into her outstretched arms, his mouth closing over hers, hot and wet. The scent of rose water encompassed him, and her lips tasted of passion and lust. Her full breasts thrust against his chest as her hand drifted lower to cover the bulge in his breeches.

"I am going to give you something that no other can."

Her eyes glinted and in a trick of the night, he imagined them red. He blinked, and when he looked again her eyes were as previous—no more than overly bright turquoise in the moonlight.

"What could I want that you are not already offering?" His lips touched the small pulse beneath her ear. A pulse, which was unusually low, a pulse, which did not...beat... He pulled back. This time her eyes *were* red, and they burned in the darkness. He tried to speak, but his words stuck in his throat. Her breath came in a foul-smelling hiss of decay and death, and fear washed over him in a red hot shiver. Her arms encircled him in bands of steel. He tried to pull away, to break her hold, but his efforts only made her smile.

"Too late, my pet. You are mine."

He brought up his knee, aimed at her stomach, but she twisted, grasped him by the forearms, and slammed him with uncommon strength into the wall. His breath left him in a rush, and he sagged to his knees only to rear back as moonlight glistened on the two, pointed, canine teeth protruding from her mouth.

He knew true fear—it was neither hot nor cold, it was chillingly numb.

Sweat trickled down his back, and his heart slapped against his ribs.

Gone was the beautiful woman he had followed into the alley. In her place, a hideous creature of the night. Rock hard agony struck his body as she lifted him without effort and sank her teeth into his neck.

Pain tore him from the trance, and he brought his fists down into her head, but her hold was a tourniquet, he a puppet and she the master. All too soon the struggle became a chore and his pain died to a dull ache.

His blood draining from his body, lethargy setting in.

He was dying, powerless to stop the creature that held him.

His soul lifted from his body, and he floated, dreamlike in a stark azure sky. Weightless, his spirit soared, beneath the clouds then above, and all that was or had ever been flashed before him.

He hovered in a meadow filled with mauve-blue heather, watching himself as a babe suckling his mother's breast. The scene changed. He was a boy of twelve, kneeling at her bedside. A baby cried and he held his mother's hand as her soul slipped from her body. Years raced by in quick succession: his first horse, his sister's fifth birthday, the joining of his first men's club, and the coming-of-age ball his father had thrown him, his first woman, and so it went on...until he settled into a sea of darkness with only a faint beacon of light in the distance.

"Vincent." Someone called him. "Vincent, you will wake."

Too much trouble. His eyelids were too heavy. He had to find the end of the tunnel, had to reach the light.

"Vincent you will open your eyes, or you will die. Do you wish that?"

"No." The words expelled in a whisper.

"Open your eyes."

He was cold, freezing. He lifted one eyelid then the other. A woman stroked his face. A woman with hair the color of a raven's wing.

"Vincent, do you know my name?"

He tried to think, but his head spun. Did he know her? His temples throbbed and he wanted to vomit but could not move his head. She leaned down and peered into his face.

Epatha! Yes! Eyes red as blood flashed in her beautiful face, and pain. Such pain. His!

"You have a choice, Vincent. A choice I do not offer lightly. You can die, or you can live. Live like me, a child of the night, beautiful, unassailable, immortal.

This is the choice I offer, but only if you vow to be mine. To be bound to me forever, be my eternal mate. I have studied you, Vincent. Watched you from the shadows. We are alike, you and I—strong, decisive, inflexible, and egocentric." She gave a short laugh. "Together, we will complete each other. Do what we want when we want. Rule this world."

"I want to live." His answer came in a whisper. Exhaustion overtook him. Death called to him. His thoughts scattered and indecisive.

"Of course, you want to live, my darling, but do you understand what I am saying?"

His eyelids fluttered. "Yes." Darkness washed over him, deep, steadfast…

"Then you promise in blood." She slashed a long nail across her wrist and dribbled a few drops of the life-giving elixir into his mouth. "A promise that cannot be broken."

Vincent gagged as salty metallic liquid touched his tongue. He attempted to spit, but she held her wrist to his lips and more of the fluid flowed into his mouth.

"You are mine. Drink—you will grow strong. You will live."

He ached to turn his head, but his strength faltered. He gulped as the blood invaded his mouth. He had little choice but to submit. Then he wanted nothing more, the blood a sweet elixir on his tongue. Euphoria washed through him and over him as the liquid reached his vital organs and his limbs began to strengthen.

Life! He was alive, whole.

The colors of the night surrounded him crystal clear. He noted all and everything with infinite detail and clarity. From the cracked pavement of the alley floor to every crevice in the wall, and the black and red bugs that crawled within. The stench of refuse, from the open sewer they had passed a block away, filled his nostrils. The pounding heart of a dog crouching in terror in a doorway five feet away was painful to his ears, and the bald patch on the back of the rat scuttling along the bottom of the wall near his left boot was easily discernible.

The taste of blood was no longer repellent, but a magical potion for which he craved. He grasped Epatha's arm hard, almost cruelly, and sucked strong and deep, drawing more of her dark elixir into his mouth as his burning hunger raged.

"No more." She pulled back, but he clung to her, taking, feasting.

"Enough, I said!" She shoved him away, and he fell heavily to the side and rolled onto his elbow to stare up at her.

She pushed to her feet, stumbling in her haste. "No more." She growled, straightening.

He wiped a hand across his lips, watching the blood trickle down her arm and pool on the ground at her feet. Hunger gnawed at his gut. Sweet blood called to him. "I want more." He needed more. Slowly, he inched toward the dark stain on the cobblestones. He felt strong, but not strong enough. He put his face to the ground and licked the blood from the stone.

"Stop that!" She kicked him back with her high, buckled-boot. "You are not a beast. Stop behaving like one."

He glared up at her and saw her draw her tongue across the wound in her arm. The cut healed over. He could taste the blood on his tongue and thirsted. Blood was a drug that clouded his brain and filled him with elation.

"Come." She held out her hand.

He took it and rose shakily to his feet, almost stumbling.

She grasped his arm, held it fast, and peered down the alleyway. "I must get you to your townhouse. Soon you will sleep. My blood will only sustain you for so long. When you wake up, your hunger will rage. Then we will feast, and you will know what it is like to be immortal!" Her eyes glowed. "You have servants at your townhouse?"

He nodded, then his lips curved to a slow smile.

"Good." She ran her tongue along her berry-red mouth and took his arm. The ruby pendant at her throat burned blood red.

Chapter One

How does one keep one's faith,
when one's soul is lost?
Present day
June

Rain-slicked cobblestones glistened beyond the tall paned window as Vincent glanced down into the narrow street. A late carriage rattled past, its candle lantern casting an eerie glow upon the lone occupant.

"The weather has changed for the worse," he remarked, dropping the velvet curtain back into place, turning to Lady Charlotte. "I fear I was too hasty in dismissing my driver for the night."

Lady Charlotte Wilkes lay on the bed with a sultry look in her azure blue eyes. "Come, Vincent, I grow tired, and Henry's meeting with Lord North will only last for so long. We have so little time together." She smiled coyly and lowered her dark lashes to accentuate her pale cheeks and golden locks. She was young, beautiful, and intelligent. How could any man resist her?

He slipped off his buckled shoes and unbuttoned his breeches.

A wild hawk screeched outside, and Vincent sprang upright in bed. He was still in his self-made purgatory, existing like a frightened child in the miner's cabin he'd called home for almost ten years. And Charlotte, a fleeting memory of a life that was all but a dream.

He slumped back on his bunk and turned over, staring blankly at the sagging rafters, imagining talons soaked in blood as the hawk outside ripped into the rabbit's back, its small life snuffed out. Oh, to have the freedom of a hawk. There were so many things he would do differently.

Stretching his arm out to the waning stream of sunlight creeping through the gap in the cabin wall, he held it still and waited for the first sting of pain to denote his existence. A red welt streaked his skin where the sun touched and he changed angle, the sunlight forming a cross on his arm. The only cross he would ever bear.

A minute more and his flesh would blister. Then what? Would his wrist sever and drop crudely to the floorboards, leaving a bloody stump? Would his body combust in a ball of flame, turn to ash as he had read long ago? Would he die? Bring an end to his miserable life—if it could even be described as such. He didn't deserve to live, but the instinct to survive was ingrained in him and he could not bring himself to end his existence.

Cursing himself for a coward, he dragged his arm from the sun and watched the flesh heal. Not a scar, nor a sting of pain to tell the tale of the burning.

Soon it would be nightfall, the tediousness of his existence broken only by the choosing of a victim for his nightly repast. He crossed his arms over his chest, closed his eyes against the gray light in the cabin, and sank into a sleep of profound blackness that only one of the undead could induce.

He awoke sometime later to the soft scurrying of a rat across his leg.

The rodent squealed, breaking the silence as it was snatched by a hand it never saw coming. He held the rodent by the tail as it struggled for freedom. Rat, rabbit, deer, moose, the occasional sheep from the paddock at the edge of the woods—he fed on all things furry. "I think not." The thought of another drop of animal blood made his stomach rebel. "This is your lucky night, my friend. You get to die a normal death." In a fluid motion, his hand ran down the rat's back, and its small bones cracked. He hurled it across the cabin to strike the wall.

How long had it been? He pushed into a sitting position on the crude cot he called his bed and leaned against the rough log wall. How long since he had ventured from the surrounding woods? The miles of tall sentinels outside his door made him claustrophobic. How long would he be forced to endure the isolation of this self-made hellhole? How long since he tasted the blood of a human? He squirmed as he imagined the sweet, salty taste upon his tongue, smooth as any good wine, the elixir of the dark life. A tingling in his gums had him concentrating hard on bringing his hunger under control.

It was too dangerous in the city, too much new technology. It was no longer safe for one of his kind. Then there was Epatha. While he lived his solitary existence, moving from one obscure haunt to the next, the heinous bitch left him alone. It was only when he tried to merge back into society and make a life for himself that she would strike.

Would her insidious revenge ever be satisfied? Couldn't she understand he was not the same man she had sired?

****

"Don't answer back, girl."

Alara cringed and braced herself for the slap she knew would come.

The blow caught her on the side of her face, as painful as ever. Her head snapped back, and two powerful hands clamped her shoulders, shoving her against the cupboard. He held her there for several minutes, rage contorting his face, then released her. She collapsed in a crumpled heap on the floor. His boot struck her ribs. Numbing pain raced through her body, and stars flashed before her tightly closed eyes.

He knelt beside her. She could smell his whiskey breath as he stroked her hair.

"You'll be a good girl now, won't you, Lara?"

Alara nodded, knowing it was the only action that would end her pain, and the ringing in her head.

She cupped her ears, and something warm and furry brushed across her left hand.

She opened her eyes.

She was in her apartment in Seattle, curled up in the corner of her bedroom on the cold hard boards, but at least they were her boards, not the worn floorboards in her foster parent's house.

Her Siamese cat nuzzled her face. She laughed, the sound more like a groan as she stroked Jesse's back. The cat arched and stretched beneath her touch.

A sense of warmth and safety flowed over Alara. She was no longer fifteen and in the power of an abusive foster father. He could no longer hurt her. Only in her dreams, and that too, she was working on with Sarah, the police psychiatrist, her closest friend next to Sam.

Sam's thirtieth must have been a doozey. She couldn't remember a thing. How had she got so drunk? She hated alcohol with a passion. She hated the stink of it. She hated that she couldn't remember now and how the alcohol could never make her forget the things she really wanted to forget. She crossed to her bed to study the covers. Who had brought her home? The coverlet was barely rumpled, the bed hadn't been slept in, but it had been slept upon. Someone who knew her had brought her home, known where to find the extra blankets in the closet, and had thrown one over her. She released the breath she'd been holding. Probably Sam, and he'd give her another ribbing when she got to work.

She stripped off her skin-tight red cocktail dress and crawled beneath the sheets. Morning was time enough to think. She closed her eyes and sank into blessed oblivion.

****

The pickup bumped along the overgrown track. Fog lights pierced the darkness and painted the trees on the perimeter of Mount Rainier National Park in harsh black relief. Lance slid a sideways glance at Jimmy. Despite the two subwoofers belting out the latest techno, the atmosphere in the sonic blue cab was tense.

"Come on, Jimmy, you're still not sore at me about the old man, are you?"

Jimmy wiped a hand across his mouth and tossed his last empty can out the window. "Still don't know why you had to kill him."

"You saw. He came at me with a knife. And you

got what you wanted, didn't you? Enough money to see you through college for the next four years."

Jimmy remained silent, staring out the side window into the night. Sure, he wanted the money, but he hadn't wanted the old man dead. If he'd only known Lance's true nature, he would never have agreed to his plan. How could he face his parents again, knowing he was responsible for Mr. Levenski's death?

They took a sharp corner, and a ramshackle cabin came into view through the trees. It must have been the one Lance spoke about, the one belonging to his great grandfather.

Lance drew the pickup to a screeching halt and shoved open the door. "This is it." He grabbed the navy backpack from the floor at Jimmy's feet, fished under the seat for a flashlight, and switched it on as he killed the headlights.

"You're sure this is the place? How long since anyone's been here?" Jimmy watched Lance climb from the pickup. "We can still go back. Turn ourselves in. You can say Mr. Levenski's death was an accident."

Lance slammed the passenger door and rounded the pickup in double time. Yanking open Jimmy's door, he dragged him out.

He fell heavily to his knees.

"Get up. If I'd known you were such a sissy, I wouldn't have asked you in on the job." His hand clenched on the strap of the backpack. "I don't care about the old man. He deserved to die. The old bastard shouldn't have come at me with a knife." He offered Jimmy his hand. "Now let's get inside," he cajoled. "I'm cold and I'm hungry."

Jimmy tossed Lance a surly look and pushed

slowly to his feet, ignoring the extended hand. He followed as Lance turned to pick his way up the path to the cabin. The cabin was all dark shadow and plane in the stark beam of the flashlight. Boarded windows resembled pirate patches across two black eyes. Long grass spiked through every crack of the three wooden stairs leading up to the porch. Several large white bones resembling animal skeletons littered the path. He had a bad feeling about this.

"We'll hide out here tonight. Split the money and head back into town in the morning. We better lay low for a week or so in case we were recognized."

"Recognized!" Jimmy grabbed Lance's arm as they climbed the weathered steps to the ancient porch and pulled him around to face him. "Recognized by who?"

"The old man coulda had one of those surveillance cameras set up in the shop. But don't worry. They won't know us in those Halloween masks of your sister's." He slapped Jimmy on the shoulder. "Great idea of yours."

He grunted an affirmative. "What about your dad? Won't he miss you?"

"Nah. He won't be back 'til Sunday night. He's up in Washington, probably with his mistress, for the weekend."

"And your mom?"

"She's usually so deep into a bottle she doesn't know if she's comin' or goin', let alone what I'm doin'." Lance dropped to a crouch. "That reminds me. I better get rid of these." He unzipped the backpack and pulled out two black and white rubber masks. Several bills of different denominations fell onto the old porch, but he scooped up the notes and poked them back into the backpack and zipped it across. Then, he tossed the masks into the nearby bushes and hitched the bag up over his shoulder. "Now let's see what dear old Gramps left for me in the cabin."

Slowly, he pushed on the door. It wasn't locked. The cabin was as black as pitch. The air reeked of decay and mold and something else that Jimmy couldn't recognize. He hung back, but Lance grasped his arm and dragged him in. "Stay with me."

A scratching sounded from a far corner of the cabin. "Who's there?" Lance swung the flashlight. The beam stunned three skinny rats and interrupted their feeding on a dead comrade beneath a small side table.

Jimmy took a hasty step backward. "Rats. I hate rats."

Lance pulled him farther into the cabin. "It's an oversized mouse. Don't be a girl. Besides, I'm not going back to town tonight." He dropped the backpack to the floor. "We've already been through this. Look. We'll start a fire. That'll scare away the rats. I read somewhere they don't like flames." He located the grate with his torch beam. "Just as I thought. The fireplace is stacked and ready."

Lance crossed the cabin and placed the flashlight on the floor, then scrounged in his pocket and produced a lighter.

Jimmy moved up alongside him. "I don't like this." He peered around the dark cabin. "Somethin's watchin' us. I can feel it."

Lance scowled. "Stop whining and help me with the fire. There's plenty of wood, but we need paper."

"What about the money?" He scrambled to unzip the bag. "Just the smaller ones." He thumbed through the bills. "There must be thousands in here."

"Yeah, the old guy was sure hoarding it."

He plucked a few small bills from the bag and pushed them at Lance to burn. The other boy poked them into the cracks between the wood, then pulled out his lighter and set fire to the money. Jimmy sighed. Lance had been right. He was being paranoid. Now the fire was shedding its meager light, he was more comfortable.

He had never liked the dark as a child and liked it even less now. He wished he were home, warm and safe in his bed with no stain of blood on his hands. He cast his companion a furtive glance and wished with renewed fervor that he had never laid eyes on Lance McManus.

A creak sounded on the other side of the room.

He stilled. "What was that?"

Lance snatched up the flashlight and shone it around. What he unearthed made his blood freeze and his stomach churn. He shoved his hands into his pockets to stop them from shaking.

Weak wavering light illuminated something standing in the shadows, a man, yet more beast than human. Dark matted hair hung to his shoulders, white waxen skin stretched across his nose and cheeks, and his eyes...they glowed bright red. "What is it, Lance?" Jimmy whispered.

"Quiet!" Lance pushed to his feet. "Who are you?" He brandished the flashlight like a weapon at the intruder and used his other hand to pull a large caliber pistol from the waistband of his pants. "You better get out of here. This is private property."

The man rose to his full height. In the distorted

luminosity of the flashlight and fire, he appeared seven feet tall. Ragged clothing hung upon his sparse frame.

"Wrong." His voice was deep, mesmerizing, and held a hint of steel. "This is *my* cabin. And it is you who will leave if you wish to live."

"Look, man, I don't know if you're stupid or just blind. Can't you see this?" Lance pushed the flashlight at Jimmy and waved the gun at the man. "Now get the hell out of here!"

"Yeah," Jimmy's trembling voice echoed.

"A gun?" The man laughed. "You think to frighten me with that toy?" Two pointed canines pushed through the gums at the roof of his mouth.

"What…What are you?" He swallowed.

"I think you know what I am."

Jimmy dropped to his knees. "Our Father, who art in heaven—"

"Shut up, Jimmy!" Lance nudged him with his boot.

The creature dove, the gun went off, and the bullet went wild. Jimmy was knocked to the side.

Lance screamed.

Jimmy couldn't think. He crawled away. The creature had Lance by the throat, he was… He had to get out!

Across the cabin, out the door, his hands slipped on the pickup's door handle. He hurled the flashlight, tried again, and wrenched open the door. His breath came short, sharp. The keys were in the ignition where Lance had left them. *Lance…what was that thing?* He shook his head. *Not now.* As the engine roared to life, he slammed the pickup into reverse and stomped on the gas pedal. Tires screeched and churned up gravel. He swung the pickup about, flicked on the headlights, and peered into the rear-view mirror. His blood froze.

A large gray wolf stood outside the cabin staring after him.

He pushed his foot flat to the floor, the pickup roared, and he sped into the darkness, praying that hell would not catch up with him and for Lance's mortal soul.

Chapter Two

Alara's phone alarm sang. Sun streamed through the half shut Venetian blinds and dust motes floated in the frigid morning air. She pushed a hand through her disheveled hair and peered into the cheval mirror across the room. She looked like hell and the pounding in her brain resembled the sledgehammer hacking into the pavement outside her window, competing with her alarm. She rose and switched it off.

A five-minute shower, an emergency cigarette, and a scalding cup of coffee later, she climbed into her beat up Pontiac Firebird, and after forty-five minutes of heavy traffic, arrived at the East Precinct.

After finding a parking space in the station yard, she pushed open the double glass doors, threw a quick hello to the desk sergeant, and marched down the hallway.

The room she shared with five other detectives was spacious, warm, and had seen a good twenty years of tobacco, coffee, and hard work.

Sam glanced up from reading the papers on his desk and grinned. "You look like hell, Detective Gale."

"I just climbed out of it, Detective Grayson." She poked out her tongue.

"Sleep well?"

"Thanks for putting me to bed."

"How did you know?"

"Who else would be such a gentleman?"

****

Sam ran his gaze from the top of her sandy curls to her shiny boots. The dark slacks, tight navy shirt, and brown leather jacket were a far cry from the little red number she'd worn last night. The dark smudges under her green eyes were too deep, and she was way too thin. He worried about her but would never tell her. She would throw it back in his face.

Alara began her career with the Seattle Police Department six years ago and in that time had seen more than the normal amount of action. He knew she liked to think she was strong, that she didn't need anyone, but deep down he feared there was a frightened little girl wishing to escape, trying to claw her way out of the cesspool she'd left behind. Finally, when achieved, perhaps she would let him get close.

He pulled a doughnut from the box on his desk. "Want one?"

"Love one." She sprung at the doughnut as he lowered it theatrically toward his mouth, snatched it before it hit his lips, and perched on the edge of his desk, taking a large bite. "So, what's new?"

"Got one of the boys from the liquor store robbery last night. You might want to speak with him."

She swallowed her bite. "Why me?"

"Just the sort of case you like. Weird. The boy drove right up to the station around three in the morning and pleaded with the desk sergeant to lock him up. Was blubbering like a baby about a monster, a vampire to be exact. Said it had torn out his friend's throat. Ever heard anything so ridiculous?" Sam watched her furtively as she barely acknowledged his words, but he knew she had been listening to every syllable from the moment he had mentioned the word vampire.

She dragged a tissue from her bag and wiped the icing from her lips. "Where is he?"

"Who?" asked Sam, signing a paper on the pile in front of him, then laying it aside.

"The boy."

"In the holding cell out back. Oh yeah, and who do you think was his partner in crime?"

She slipped from his desk and dropped her handbag onto the desk next to his. "I'm sure you'll tell me."

"Lance McManus."

"McManus? Where have I heard that name?"

"Councilor McManus. The one who is running for congressman."

Alara expelled a heavy breath. "Dammit. What did the captain say?"

"To keep it under wraps. The press will have a field day if a whisper of another copycat vampire killing gets out."

"What do you mean copycat?"

"Well, you know there's no such thing."

"You might think that, Sam, but you know my views are different." Alara headed for the door and wrenched it open. "One day I'll find him and when I do…"

"Wait, I'm with you on this one."

"Yeah. I guess you'd better be. Then I can't be accused of making up stories, can I?"

Sam knew he deserved that. Alara believed a vampire killed her childhood boyfriend, Ice. She'd sworn she'd seen a black-cloaked figure fleeing from the scene. She had visited a dozen police psychiatrists, and even now insisted she knew what she saw. It had been a vampire. But there just wasn't any such creature. And if there were, they sure as hell didn't live in Seattle. A serial killer pretending to be a vamp, maybe. Like the one who killed her second foster mother, Detective Redmond.

But a real vamp? He mentally shook his head.

He didn't think so.

****

The interrogation cell had a two-way mirror on one wall, and an old wooden table with four chairs. A large tape player sat on the edge of the table, and two uniformed police officers stood at the back of the cell behind the offender.

Chief Hendricks had met them at the holding cell informing them he wished to observe the interview.

Alara nodded and proceeded inside; Sam followed.

The boy already sat at the table. He looked terrible—thin with short brown hair and red-rimmed, blue eyes that looked sunken into his face. Sam took the seat across from the boy, and Alara perched on the chair next to him, observing as Sam began his questioning.

The boy fidgeted in his seat.

She almost felt sorry for him, but she hardened her heart. This kid had taken part in the murder of an old man who had done no more than try to defend his livelihood.

Sam switched on the recorder.

"Do you wish to have a lawyer present?" he asked.

"No."

Alara nodded and went on to question the boy over

the liquor store robbery. He named Lance as the one who shot the storeowner. They had worn Halloween masks he had taken from his sister's room. Jimmy had needed money to go to Princeton, and it had been Lance's idea to rob the store. Alara pumped him for more details, which he was only too ready to supply. It seemed the boy had worse things on his mind than going to prison.

Now came the question Alara dreaded yet thirsted for. "What happened at the cabin?"

The boy's face turned a sickly shade of white.

"Answer the question. What happened at the cabin?" Sam slammed his fist onto the table.

Jimmy remained silent, staring down at his tightly clenched hands.

"Jimmy?" Alara prompted.

"I can't. He'll know. I know he will."

"You must. We can't find Lance's killer unless you cooperate."

More silence, then the boy spoke. Slowly at first, then his words gained momentum. "When we arrived...we ditched the masks. Lance waited for me before opening the door."

"What next?" urged Alara, feeling sympathy for the boy, but at the same time wishing he would hurry.

Jimmy glanced around the room as if looking for a way to escape, before staring hard at the two-way mirror. "What if he's watching? What if he gets me?" He reached across and grabbed her hands. "You won't let him have me? You won't let him do to me what he did to Lance? He can change to a wolf. Who knows what else he can do?"

"A wolf?"

28

Alara disentangled her hands from Jimmy's and clasped them in her lap.

"A huge one. Gray," the boy elaborated.

Sam looked at her and when she didn't speak, he went on. "Tell us what happened, Jimmy. What did he do to Lance?"

"When Lance opened the door, it stunk like, well, it was kind of musty, rotten, like something dead. I didn't like it. I didn't want to go in there, but Lance insisted. The place gave me the creeps. Anyway, there was something that kept shifting in the corner. At first, we thought it was rats."

"Rats?" she prompted.

"Lance shone the flashlight and there was a dead rat. Other rats were feeding on it."

She grimaced. "What then?"

The wildness was back in the boy's eyes. He gripped the edge of the table so hard his knuckles turned white. "It was horrible—pale, thin, and its eyes, they were red. Its hair, it was like, in knots and all gross. Lance shouted for the creature to get out, but it just sat there staring. It said for us to leave, that the cabin belonged to him."

"The creature spoke?"

"Yeah. Real cultured like. Smooth. Bit of an accent. Lance pointed the gun. And…and it laughed. Laughed at the gun as if it wouldn't hurt him. As if he didn't care. Two big teeth grew down from the top of his mouth, then…"

"An accent? What sort of accent?"

Jimmy frowned. "English, maybe."

"You keep on saying, he. Are you sure it was a he?"

"As sure as I can be, under that filthy hair and ragged clothes."

"What did Lance do when the creature bared its teeth?"

"He got really mad and fired the gun—everything happened in a rush. The creature flew across the room. I heard Lance scream. The gun hit the ground with the flashlight. I heard a choking sound, looked up, and in the firelight saw…" Jimmy buried his head in his arms. "I wanted to stay, but I couldn't. It would've got me too." He looked up. Tears stained his cheeks. "I had to leave,. You can see that, can't you?"

"You did the right thing." Alara patted his hand.

"You're gonna get it—that thing that killed Lance. Right?"

"We're not even sure Lance is dead." Sam leaned back and crossed his arms. "But yes, we will do our utmost. Can you lead us to the cabin?"

The boy's expression closed over and he shook his head. "No. No, I'm not going back there. You can't make me."

"If it is a vampire, they don't like the daylight. Isn't that so, Detective Gale?" Sam looked pointedly at Alara.

"That's right, Jimmy. From what I've read on vampires they explode in sunlight or turn to ash." She threw Sam a look, searching for a smirk, but whatever he was thinking his expression remained bland. "We need to recover the money. If we can get the money back, the district attorney might be prepared to make a deal."

"I told them last night; the money is in the cabin."

"All the more reason for you to take us there."

Jimmy sighed and nodded, then his jaw clenched. "Fine, but you'd better take a fuckin' big stake."

****

A shiver ran down Alara's spine at first sight of the cabin through the trees. Could this be the place Ice's killer had hidden all these years? It wasn't anything out of the norm, just an ordinary cabin, the same as thousands of others, just a little more dilapidated. The unmarked car took the last bump in the dirt track and came to a halt. Two police cars pulled up behind it. She slipped from the car, drew her pistol, and waited for Sam and Jimmy to follow.

Jimmy held back with one of the uniformed officers and Sam drew his Glock 19 and led the way up the overgrown path.

She noted several large, white bones strewn across the ground as they moved, and heard Sam mention something about moose and sheep. He climbed the steps beside her, and she set her foot to the rotted door. It crashed back on its hinges and fell inward with a thud, churning up dust. They moved into the cabin simultaneously, guns ready and pointed, followed by three forensic officers.

Nothing.

Well, nothing except one very dead body, several small bones, and a few sticks of rotted furniture, but certainly no vampire.

She lowered her gun. She didn't know what she expected. To find the vampire lying in a coffin in the corner, just like in the movies. She gave a short laugh.

Nothing had been done to conceal the crime. Lance's pale, lifeless body was in a crumpled heap where he'd fallen. Little blood, just a few drops the creature missed. Several bills lay scattered on the floor, but the backpack Jimmy described was gone.

The boy was right. The place stank. It reeked of death. Several dead rats lay in the corner in different stages of decay.

If a vampire held up in this cabin, rats and animals would have been his only source of sustenance, but he'd have had to be good at avoiding the sunlight streaming through the cracks in the walls.

She knelt to examine the body. Two dark puncture wounds, two inches apart, just like Ice...

Ice, who had taken her from the streets, given her a home, loved her like no other. It had been a small apartment on the worst side of town, but it had been theirs. Then came the night of the robbery. She hadn't wanted him to go. She hadn't liked the sound of the job, and she'd never liked Roule. He'd been a bully and a thug, but Ice had owed him. Owed him for her!

The robbery had gone horribly wrong. The police were tipped off. Ice was wounded. Blood, there had been so much blood. She had dragged him into the back of the shop to rest and tried to pass herself off as a girl who worked in the store. The storekeeper's body lay at her feet beneath the counter, and Roule had left them to take the rap.

There came a cry from the back. The police pushed passed her, and Ice...Ice lay on the floor, his throat torn. Two puncture wounds in his neck. She ran to the window and saw him, a creature in a black cloak, fleeing along the alley...

Sam touched her arm. "Are you all right?"

She straightened. "Of course, I'm all right. It's not like I haven't seen this sort of thing before." She glanced at the forensics people dusting the cabin for prints, and the CSI team gathering the little evidence left at the scene.

"Detective Gale?" A uniformed officer stood at her side. "We'd like to move the body now."

"Did you find anything?"

"We're still working on it, but this is what we have so far." The officer showed her the contents of several small evidence bags containing an old piece of torn cloth, several bills in varying denominations, and a tarnished key."

"A key," she murmured. "What would a vampire be doing with a key? And a key to what?"

Sam pulled on a rubber glove and took the brown paper bag from the officer for a better inspection of the key. He tipped it out onto his palm. "It could be nothing. The key could have belonged to the previous owner of the cabin."

She moved closer. "Or it could belong to him."

"Whoever he is." Sam met her gaze.

"It could be a safe deposit box key. It might lead us to his identity." Her hands shook in her coat pockets. Could this be the clue she had searched for all these years?

Sam dropped the key back into the bag and handed it to the officer, then turned for the door. "Coming?"

She nodded, but as she turned, she spied a small shiny object in the corner of the room, glinting in the sunlight streaming through the cabin wall. She would have missed it, had she not noticed the rat watching her with quiet interest from beneath the ancient single bed. The object lay beside the rat. She dropped to her knees and scrambled under the bed to discover a chain and locket as the rodent scampered away.

Turning the piece of jewelry over, she brought the heart-shaped locket closer to her face to read the delicate flowery script. *To Annabelle, Forever, V.*

Alara tucked it into her breast pocket, heart racing, her hands shaking. For the first time in her career, she was concealing evidence, but this was yet another clue to Ice's death and she would not let it pass. Surely, there could not be more than one vampire in the world. And this time she had something personal, something that would bring her closer to knowing him. And who was Annabelle, a mother, a lover, a sweetheart, or just another victim?

"I think, Detective Gale, that might be illegal. In fact, I'm downright sure of it."

Alara swung to find Sam behind her, a condemning look on his lean face.

"I'm taking it back to the station for evidence," she defended, striding past him.

"Then why don't you give it to Sergeant Ryan?" he questioned, following.

She stopped outside the door on the porch, staring blankly into the trees. "I will, but later. It's my only link, Sam." She turned to face him. "Understand? I have been waiting so long."

"Then let me help you." He touched her arm.

"I will." She pulled away, severing the connection between them, and took the three steps in a bound.

He followed her to flat ground, keeping his distance. "The weekend then, no more, or I will have to report you." He said it with a glint in his eyes, but she knew he was serious.

She nodded and knelt to examine the roped off area

at her feet. "I'd probably do the same. I guess that's why we're cops." She held his gaze. "It'll be in evidence on Monday."

He crouched beside her and gave a quick smile. "Good girl. But wouldn't it be easier to hand it in then check it back out after it's been marked down for evidence?"

"Right again. I'm too close to this case. It's making me jittery. I'll hand the locket in when I get back to the station. Now," she said examining the sectioned off piece of ground. "What about Jimmy's wolf?"

Sam rose and stretched his back. "From reading the signs, the animal stood here and watched Jimmy drive away as the boy stated. Then it disappeared into the cabin, came out, and headed north through the forest."

"North? Toward Seattle?"

Sam nodded. "But the country's pretty rugged through there. We wouldn't stand a chance of tracking it."

"After the boy, do you think?"

"Couldn't say." Sam shrugged. "Perhaps he just didn't want to stick around and wait for the police to show up."

"He had no way of knowing if the boy would go to the police."

"Didn't he? I thought these creatures read minds?"

Alara frowned. "Not sure about that, but I guess if I saw a friend's throat ripped out it might be the first place I'd go. Who else could protect him?" She looked around, finding Jimmy already settled in the squad car. One police officer sat in the front, another standing outside the car door. She turned back to Sam. "The wolf went inside for the money. We didn't find it, and

Jimmy didn't take it with him."

Sam shook his head. "I know what you're saying, but it's illogical. A wolf carrying a backpack. There must be another explanation."

"Then you explain it. There are no human tracks other than Lance and Jimmy's."

Sam grimaced and raised his gaze to the heavens, then he looked Alara in the eyes. "That is the insane part. I can't."

****

Rain sifted down from a black sky distorting Vincent's view of the doorway across the road. Rain. It seemed it always rained on the important events in his life. It rained the night he had met Epatha, and she changed his life forever. It rained the night the Native American shaman had cursed him and condemned him to a living hell, and it rained on the night of his parting from Epatha.

France 1877. Irate townspeople had trapped him and Epatha in a tavern. Really, it was the excuse for which he had been searching. After his cursing by the shaman, he could no longer abide Epatha's insatiable appetite for the blood of the young. He suggested they separate and meet on the docks. They had been talking of returning to Italy. She agreed. They leapt from the windows in the tavern to the alley below and fought their way through several townsfolk gathered with guns and swords. Vincent managed to break free, stole a horse, and kept riding.

Hiding out during the daylight in an abandoned chalet, that night he set sail on a ship to the West Indies, thankful to be parted from Epatha before she discovered his lack of blood lust. He had known should she find out his secret, it would be down to him or her. He was growing weaker from lack of blood and finding it harder to keep his secret from her. He knew he had no other option but to escape.

It also rained the night he met Annabelle. His beautiful Annabelle, the only woman he ever loved. And a storm unlike any other had raged the night Epatha finally tracked him down and exacted her revenge, by taking Annabelle's life.

Music, loud and intrusive, distorted by the night traffic, issued from the nightclub as the door opened. That, accompanied by the stench of humanity, served to bring him from his dark thoughts.

Neon blue and yellow winked at him from across the road, *Tommy's Nightclub & Grill.* If he concentrated enough, he could hear the rapid pounding of heartbeats, filling the night with their symphony of sound. And here he was, huddled like a piece of vermin in a refuse laden alley, waiting for an unsuspecting soul to emerge from the nightclub to step into his parlor, like a fly to a spider. He hated it. He hated himself for the low creature he had become. Yes, he possessed superhuman strength and speed when called upon, the ability to shape shift to a wolf, or to dissolve into mist, but what use was that when it only served to better evil's end?

He laughed. *How ironic. A vampire who can feel emotion—remorse, love, sorrow, hate.* He felt it all and it ate at his insides.

A curse placed upon him when he took the life of a Cheyenne chief.

Even now he could see his dark eyes accusing, staring up at him in death, felt the bludgeon across his head, and the pain when he had awoken to find himself trussed like a sacrificial turkey before a roaring fire. Seven painted braves stood around him, and before him, an old Native American shaman sat, mumbling unintelligible words. Held by four braves, a bitter concoction forced down his throat, and again he had passed out. When he'd surfaced, he was no longer bound, and his memory temporarily obliterated. The shaman spoke then, in stilted English. He told Vincent he had spared him death, but he would soon wish he had not. For every soul taken would haunt him for the rest of his many days. Then the visions started, flashing through his mind so fast he thought he would go insane—blood, torture, the faces, the screams.

He'd staggered into the forest, and that was where Epatha found him, but he never told her what happened.

Even now the face of his father flashed before his eyes. He had always been a God-fearing man, his father. And on looking into the face of his demon son, he had dropped to his knees and prayed... But Vincent would not think of that now. It was long past, and to dwell on matters more than two centuries old would serve no purpose other than to drive him to madness.

No. What he would do tonight had to be done. To give him strength. He needed time to think. Time to gather his wits, time for his body to rejuvenate and become whole again and cast aside the wretched creature who had spent the seventy-five years since Annabelle's death crawling from one ancient haunt to another. Or should he say running? He would enter society, take back his life, and if Epatha should surface, this time he would kill her.

He saw three young men and a woman emerge

from the nightclub across the road. A youth around twenty, with spiky brown hair and baggy clothing, swayed slightly on his feet as he spoke, and started to back away.

"Nah, you go ahead. I told Kate I'd pick her up from work. I'll be there next time." His voice echoed into the night.

"Sure?"

"Yeah. She'll kill me if I'm late. She hates waiting on nights like this. Creeps her out. My car is parked in the next block. I'll take a shortcut through the alley. Need a piss anyway." He emphasized the fact by cupping himself.

The young woman next to him laughed and moved to hug the arms of the other two men. After a hasty goodnight, the group parted and the other three headed off, leaving the youth to cross the road.

Vincent watched, his back pressed to the wall, hidden in the shadows, alert and ready.

Chapter Three

Charlie shook his head, trying to clear his mind, wishing he hadn't drunk that last bourbon. He'd promised Kate he'd pick her up. If he was late his sister would have his balls for sure.

He tripped on the curb, swore loudly, then laughed. "Can't even walk, Charles," he mimicked his sister's voice.

He crossed the road and hesitated.

He had taken this alley a hundred times, plastered and sober, but for some reason tonight it looked darker, threatening, as if something lurked within the shadows.

He laughed again. "Get a grip, Charlie. Of course, there's nothing in there." He took a deep breath and stepped into the alley. The thick, heavy smell from the rotting garbage had to be fish and it took everything he could muster not to barf on his own shoes. Shaking his head to keep the smell at bay, he unzipped his fly, sighing as he relieved himself, trying hard not to breathe too deeply. Finally done, he zipped back up and walked on.

In the distance, he noticed the faint light from the back of D'Omeco's Spaghetti Bar. He'd just head for the light and he'd be fine. Three more steps and his boot caught on the pavement, and he staggered. The cold air had really hit him hard. His head felt crammed with cotton candy, all sticky and grainy with no clear thoughts. He'd have one hell of a hangover come morning. Damn Scuddy for supplying him with that fake ID and shooting him that last drink. He'd said he didn't want it, but Lucy had laughed, and she was so hot.

He stopped and leaned against the wall, his stomach turning cartwheels. He was certain a bass drum had taken up residence in his skull. He coughed, leaned forward, and spewed his dinner all over the cobblestones. Now he knew he shouldn't have had that last drink. Charlie kept his head down, sweat beading his forehead, and dragged a hand across his mouth. Clearing his throat, he spat and straightened.

Yet, the feeling of being watched persisted. The alley, in black shadow, and rain drizzling from steely clouds overhead. He lurched onward. It was as if he was being compelled to move. He didn't want to go forward, but he couldn't go back. He was drawn like a moth to the light up ahead, and he was already late to get Kate, so he rushed on.

The glow from the restaurant grew brighter as he neared. A man emerged from the back, threw something into the dumpster, and disappeared back inside. Charlie expelled a ragged breath and berated himself for jumping at shadows.

Then from the darkness shot a hand.

Slammed into the alley wall, all breath was expelled from his lungs. Lifted from the ground, his feet dangled helplessly beneath him. A face hovered—white, grotesque, with matted black hair. All thoughts of Kate vanished. But when the man didn't move, Charlie's bravado returned, and his squeamishness disappeared.

"Is this a joke?" He turned his head the best he could to look around. "If Scuddy put you up to this I'll…" He stared the man in the eye. "What are you?" He frowned. "A Goth. I…geez, you stink."

Two teeth protruded from the man's top gums.

"Scuddy! All right, you've had your fun!" Charlie's voice sounded strained even to his own ears. His words hung in the silence. No one jumped from the shadows, and he was forced to acknowledge that this wasn't a joke after all.

"Fine," he tried for a steadier tone, "say this isn't a joke and you are for real, this is even better." He wriggled trying to loosen his captor's grip. "You're going to make me like you aren't you, but not so ugly, I hope."

****

Vincent's eyes narrowed. Of all the things he had expected from the boy, this bravado was the last. "You are not afraid of me?"

The boy grinned. He actually grinned. Never had Vincent seen this before in all his ages.

"Nah, not really. What are you going to do? Drink my blood?" The lad mimicked in his best Bela Lugosi voice.

Vincent frowned. He'd seen one or two vampire movies over the years, just to stay abreast of what had become of his friend, Bram Stoker's, work. They had collaborated on *a certain vampire story* for many long nights over quite a few glasses of red. It was unfortunate Bram's work had never really been appreciated until after his death, but his widow had reaped a pretty reward.

Vincent shrugged, returned to the present and the

lad squirming in his grip. He lowered the boy to the ground, keeping an iron hold on his shoulders. He could hear the boy's blood pumping through his veins, the heat radiating from his skin. One of his long teeth pricked his lip and his blood tasted metallic on his tongue, but something made him hesitate from taking the boy's life.

"Gee, man, you really need a haircut, and you stink like a skunk. I thought it was the dumpster, but—"

"I get the picture." His voice held an edge. Did the boy have no idea that his life hung in the balance?

"You didn't answer my question." The boy stopped wriggling. "Are you real? I mean, I don't believe in vamps, but it would be way cool." The boy seemed to hesitate. "You're not one of those weird serial killers, are you? I mean, if you were real, it would be so great. Do vampires really live forever?"

"Enough!"

"But—"

"Cease your prattling and let me get this over with! I have no choice. I need blood." He made to lower his teeth toward the boy's neck, his canines fully extended, but the boy forced his arms up between them. He held Vincent a fraction from his throat.

"Hey, man, chill. I can help!"

"Yes, by letting me drink you." Vincent knew he could have the boy with ease, but for some uncanny reason he hesitated. The lad intrigued him.

"If it's blood you want, I can get it. All you want, as much as you want."

Vincent drew back a few inches, but held the boy pinned to the wall. "Oh, yes. How?"

"My sister."

"You are going to feed me your sister?" Vincent did not like the sound of this. Anyone who would feed his sister to a vampire deserved to die.

"No! My sister works at the local blood bank. I was on my way to pick her up. If you wait here, I'll get the key. I know where she keeps it. I can break into the bank and steal you a couple of pints."

He stared into the boy's eyes. Could he trust him? It had been so long since he had trusted anyone, and this was a new time, a different time. He did not know the caliber of people that now populated the cities. However, he was tired and growing weaker by the moment. "You could tell the police."

"I could." The boy rushed on. "But I won't. If I did, you couldn't make me like you." He grinned. "It would be awesome. I could be like that rock star vampire in that Lestat movie. And the chicks…wow, imagine how many girls you could…" He looked away. "Meet over a lifetime?"

He wanted to smile at the boy's misconstrued idea of a vampire, but the matter was too serious. He was not inclined to kill the boy. He wanted to believe in him. He wanted to trust again. He needed to feel…something. He lowered the boy until his tiptoes touched the ground. He knew he was a fool, but he released him anyway and the lad staggered back. "Very well, one hour. But betray me, and I will track you down. There will be no place you can hide. Understand?"

The boy nodded and took off into the darkness.

****

Vincent knew he shouldn't have trusted the boy. He had waited for over two hours, in the numbing rain on the corner of the alleyway. Several insignificant beings milled around the entrance of the nightclub, but no other ventured across the road and into the alley.

The spaghetti bar closed long ago, and he knew he would not track the boy down as he had stated. There would always be closer prey. The alleys in the cheap side of town would be a hive of human vermin. He knew he should have tried there first, but the glitzy lights and thumping music of the club had drawn him in. A fact he now regretted.

The street at the entrance to the alley was in full shadow, the nearest streetlight more than twenty feet away. In a fit of perversity, he rounded the corner and leaned against the brick wall to watch the goings on across the road.

A lone girl strode from the nightclub toward the sidewalk, and he straightened. He didn't know what it was about her, perhaps the air of solitude she wore like a cloak. He could see it in the aura that surrounded her. In the tilt of her chin, in the way she looked at none of the people around her. She wanted to be alone. She needed no one, just like him. She was slim, not at all to his taste. He favored voluptuous women.

She wore a pair of hip-hugging, low riding jeans, and her top consisted of a piece of olive-green cloth stretched across her small breasts. That in itself did things to him he had forgotten existed for decades, and it had nothing to do with the blood lust, which pervaded his body.

A riot of sandy curls hung barely to her shoulders, framing a slender, oval face. He could have sworn her eyes were green as they stared across at him. He knew she couldn't see him clearly, yet still she looked as if she tried to penetrate the shadows, infiltrate the night, look into his soul.

A moment later, a yellow cab came to a screeching halt beside her, and his lonely girl was gone.

"Hey, man, are you still there?"

Vincent watched the cab pull away from the curb and disappear into traffic and the busy Seattle night, then he turned back into the alley.

"You are late."

"Yeah, sorry 'bout that." Charlie gave a nervous laugh. "Almost got caught by one of my sister's friends. Had to come up with an excuse about picking up some of Kate's files. Brenda, that's Kate's friend, waited while I retrieved them from her office then walked me to the door. Had to make sure she was gone before I tried again. Hope she doesn't mention she saw me." Charlie swung a backpack from his shoulder to the ground and pulled the zipper open. From within, he lifted a large tube of blood and tossed it to Vincent.

He caught it and felt the roof of his mouth tingle and swell but remained hesitant. Blood in a bag? Was the boy toying with him?

"Well, aren't you gonna drink? You're a vamp, aren't you? This wasn't some kind of sick joke after all..." Charlie frowned. "It better not..."

Vincent fumbled with the bag. "How?"

"I dunno. Rip off the top or somethin'. You've got sharp teeth; bite it."

Vincent's canines broke through his top gum. He looked down at Charlie then at the tube in his hand. It was dark in the alley, but he could see the sparkle of the boy's eyes as he watched him. The lad's blood would be easier, faster.

His gaze focused on the boy's throat, and he lifted the bag and punched his teeth into the tube.

Blood spurted over his face, his hands, and ragged clothes, but some did manage to find its way to his mouth. The first taste was relief and satisfaction—like sweetmeat after a famine. He sighed.

"Are you gonna make me a vamp now?"

He did not acknowledge the boy's words but continued licking the last dregs of blood from the bag and his fingers, then he scooped the next plastic tube from Charlie's backpack. He could see the boy grimacing as he heard the squelching noise of the second tube being emptied but he had no time for the boy's sensibilities. Already he was changing. His chest felt thicker, his shoulders broader. The blood from the boy at the cabin had given him only strength enough to journey to the city, not enough to regenerate his skin tissue. He'd starved himself almost to emaciation, living off animals and birds. Too long he had thought he had wanted to die. Now all he could think of was regaining his strength and joining the populated world. This time he would find Epatha. This time, one of them would not live through the battle.

With the third tube, he managed to pull off the small top and squirt the blood in a more uniform fashion into his mouth. His canines retracted with subsiding hunger, and his limbs stronger than they had been in years. He wiped his soiled hands down his filthy linen shirt. "I will need clothes."

"I thought you'd say that." Charlie dragged an oversized blue and yellow T-shirt and a pair of baggy khaki shorts from the backpack and tossed them to Vincent.

The only light in the alley came from the nightclub, and the pale moonlight above, but he detected the colors clearly. The same way he could tell Charlie had spiked brown hair, large trusting pale-blue eyes and wore an orange top with a white logo splashed across the front, saying Bon Jovi. He wondered what a Bon Jovi was but passed on to Charlie's khaki shorts like those he had pressed on Vincent. They hung from the boy's slim hips and had multiple pockets.

Dragging his ripped shirt over his head, he dropped it to the ground and slipped on the shirt he'd been given. Plenty of room, but he gathered that was the fashion from what he observed of the males across the road. He had been in hiding a long time. "I see fashion has changed a lot in seventy years."

Charlie shrugged, but said nothing, and Vincent stripped off his rotted pants and pulled on those that Charlie had supplied. They came to his calves, and he raised a brow.

"Not too bad. A little snug, but they'll do. Here, you better put this on 'til you can get a haircut." Charlie pushed a black woolen cap into his hand and Vincent studied it, then catching Charlie staring, dragged the hat down over his matted hair and tucked the rest up beneath. He would have loved to see himself in a mirror. He suspected he looked frightening. But it had been long since he held the pleasure of his own reflection and knew he never would again.

"I was thinking." Charlie zipped up the bag and came to his feet. "Since you're not from around here…" He looked away, as if uncomfortable with what he was about to say. "…you don't know this town like I do."

Vincent crossed his arms over his chest. "Go on,"

he urged with a hint of impatience.

"Well, I was thinking of taking you home, but Kate would probably think you were some kind of homeless guy and try and kick you out." He dug his wallet out of his back pocket and pulled it open. "If I had money, I could get you a room, but…" He stuck his finger in his wallet and dragged it along the empty bill slot. "As you can see, I'm a bit short. No money 'til Friday."

Vincent swept up his old trousers from the ground, stuck his hand into the back pocket, and pulled out a fistful of one-hundred-dollar bills. He grasped Charlie's hand and slapped them into his palm, some of the money spilling to the ground. "Is this enough?"

Charlie frowned and scooped up the money from the alley floor. "I can't see properly in this light. Can I take it across the road?"

Vincent hesitated.

"I'll come back, promise." Charlie backed away.

Vincent nodded. He couldn't help but like the boy.

Charlie raced out of the alley and across the road into the light of the streetlamp. He peered down at the money in his hand, and a wide grin spread across his face. He raced back. "Where did you get this?" he asked panting. "Have any more?"

"Is it enough?"

"Well, yeah, more than enough. But—"

"Then, shall we proceed?"

"But I thought you might turn me into a vamp first."

The look Vincent gifted him with quelled anything else Charlie might say. The boy opened his mouth then shut it again and with a resigned sigh led Vincent out of the alley and down the street.

However, Charlie being Charlie, his vivacious personality could not be contained for long. Soon, he was pointing out the sights of Seattle, the Needle Point Restaurant, and the Virginia Mason Medical Center to name a couple. Vincent was only too happy to listen. He preferred it rather than have the boy ask too many personal questions.

Charlie had grown up in Seattle, which he described as the most incredible city in the whole of the big U.S.A. His parents had moved to Alabama when he was fifteen, his father having taken a promotion within the insurance company for which he worked. He had begged his parents to be able to move in with his sister who had already settled into her own apartment with a job at the West Side Blood Bank. She was five years his senior.

Charlie dropped out of school at the age of seventeen to play lead guitar in a heavy metal rock band, who hoped one day to land a recording contract. During the day, he freelanced as a photographer for the *Seattle Journal*.

Several streets later, Charlie led Vincent across the road and into The Edgewater Hotel. The boy pushed through the revolving glass door in front of Vincent, marched up to the marble counter, and slammed his hand down on the silver bell. Vincent hung back, watching.

A distinguished gentleman emerged from a back room and looked at Charlie with an air of distaste. "Yes, can I help you?" He glanced over Charlie's shoulder at Vincent and his tone took on an edge.

"We do not serve drug users, sir," the man explained raising his nose in the air.

Charlie spun and glanced at Vincent, a glint of humor in his eyes, his lips quirking as if he were about to laugh, but he sobered again at Vincent's scowl and faced the clerk. "He's clean. I can vouch for him."

The look the man gave Charlie told him just what he thought of his word, but the boy refused to be deterred. He pulled out the money Vincent had supplied from his pocket and slapped it onto the counter. "Your best room. My friend will be staying for—" He swung back to Vincent.

"Four weeks."

"The room will be two hundred dollars a night," the clerk returned straight-faced.

A soft whistle escaped Charlie's lips and he spun and raised a brow. "You still want it?"

Vincent nodded.

Charlie turned back. "We'll take it."

With a resigned sigh the clerk opened the large, red leather book on the counter, and slid it toward Charlie.

"The room is for my friend."

"Then your friend must sign." The man looked down his nose again at Charlie. "If he cannot write, he can make his mark."

Vincent moved up alongside his young friend, picked up the pen and signed his name in a long flowing script. *'Vincent'*.

"Wow man, that's real cool. How did you learn to write like that?"

Vincent snapped the book closed and pushed it toward the clerk. The man opened the page and looked down at the signature.

"A surname if you please."

Vincent took the book back and signed,

'D'Armano'.

"An address." The clerk raised a dark brow.

"He just sailed in on a cargo ship," Charlie lied. "He has no address, but he can use mine. 3 Edwards Street, Seattle."

The clerk nodded and watched without comment while Vincent filled in the missing information. Finally, the man handed Vincent a small plastic card, taking pains not to touch his hand.

"I will not be requiring room service."

"But it is stand—" The words died on the clerk's lips as he looked into Vincent's eyes. "Very well, sir, it will be as you say. I will inform the staff—"

Ignoring Charlie's presence, Vincent turned before the man stopped speaking and strode across the deep red carpet toward a winding, marble staircase at the end of the foyer. The less the boy knew about him, the less anyone knew about him, the better.

"There is an elevator to your right," called the desk clerk, as Charlie ran up alongside Vincent.

He glanced at the boy. "You can go now."

Charlie frowned "What do you mean, go? What if I don't want to go? You were going to *make* me like *you*, remember? I'm not going anywhere."

Vincent settled a look on Charlie that would have leveled a stronger man, but for some reason didn't faze the boy. He compressed his lips and followed Charlie as he led the way to the elevator.

Charlie pushed the button. "Have you been in an elevator before?"

"I have."

"You need me, anyway," the boy elaborated, not waiting for Vincent to say more as they stepped into the elevator. "And I always did want to see inside one of these posh hotel rooms. Can you believe the Village People sang in the bar downstairs after their concert? And that Bill Clinton had a rally for his first presidential election here? The crowd was so large that not everyone heard his speech in the Olympic Ballroom, so a stage was set up outside in the parking lot and he gave the speech a second time."

Vincent remained silent. He had no idea who the people were of which the boy spoke and did not care. As the elevator hit the twelfth floor and the door slid open, he stepped out onto the carpeted hallway. He needed a shower and exhaustion weighed on his shoulders, though he reasoned the boy would tire Dracula himself.

"Room 1204. Here it is." Charlie stopped in front of the door across from the elevator, and Vincent stared down at the card the clerk had supplied, trying to decipher how he would open the door with a piece of plastic. Charlie snatched the card and slid it into the silver slot. "We have to wait for the green light." The light appeared and Charlie removed the card, pushed open the door, and the light in the room switched on automatically.

"Whew, this is even better than I imagined." Charlie waited for Vincent to enter, then raced across the room to throw himself onto the king-sized bed. He rolled over, plucked the remote from the bedside table and high voltage rock belted into the silence.

He glared, and Charlie killed the music, dropped the remote onto the bed, and raced across the room to try out the overstuffed chair and footrest by the river-rock fireplace. "Wow, would you look at that view?"

The boy jumped from the armchair and leapt over the rug to peer out of the floor-to-ceiling window into the night. "Elliott Bay, and I bet you can see the Olympic Mountains come sunrise." He gasped and spun. "Sorry, man, I shouldn't have said that, should I? I mean, vampires can't look at the sun, can they?"

"They can watch the sunrise, yes, as long as they do not stand in direct sunlight."

Charlie stepped away from the window, sobering. "That money...ah, where'd you get it? I mean...you didn't murder anyone, did you?" He gave a hesitant grin.

Vincent tossed off his hat and was in the process of stripping off his shirt. He needed a shower, bad, but Charlie's words gave him pause. His hands bunched in the material, and he pulled his shirt the rest of the way over his head. He rolled it into a tight ball, and it struck the window beside the boy's head and dropped to the floor.

Charlie cringed but didn't move.

He had learned long ago that a vampire should feel no remorse, but he was no ordinary vampire. He could still see the horrified face of the boy, Lance, and feel the feeble struggle of his limbs as his blood drained.

"Where I came by the money is my business." Vincent turned for the bathroom. "I will not be questioned by you or anyone else. Put the blood in the refrigerator and see yourself out."

Charlie moved quickly and caught his arm. "Sorry, man, I—"

"I am a vampire, Charlie." He cut him off, his tone emotionless as he stared down at the boy's hand on his arm. "That is what I do. I kill people and I drink their blood. Do not make any mistake. I am ruthless and I have no emotions." He did not wait for Charlie to answer but pulled free. He strode into the bathroom and slammed the door.

Stripping off his shorts, he turned on the faucet and stepped into the first shower he'd had for almost a decade, apart from the rain in the forest on a stormy night.

The shower was as close to heaven as he would ever get, but it would never wash away the blood on his hands and in his heart.

****

He was watching her. She could feel his gaze on her, yet she was unafraid, more curious. There was something familiar about his carriage, yet he sat just enough in shadow for his face to remain unseen.

Alara had arrived at the nightclub at eleven and taken her usual seat in the corner. The band who played were midrange, not good, not bad, but would never be chart toppers.

She ordered a margarita and settled back to observe the crowd. Twenties to thirties, they fit the profile of the usual night-clubber, in their glitzy body-hugging clothes.

All except him.

He was dressed totally in black. Boots, long leather coat, open and pushed back to reveal a black shirt and dark pants. Hair, raven black, and short, and she knew he was looking.

It was not conceit, or in any way related to the fact she thought herself attractive. If anything, she was too wiry and her chest too flat. It was the strange tingly feeling that persisted in the pit of her stomach.

She turned her gaze from him and pushed through the noisy crowd to fetch another drink.

"I've been watching you all night. Wanna dance?" A lanky, well-oiled male in a bright blue shirt, hip hugging black pants, and a multitude of gold chains blocked her path. She winced as his body odor invaded her nose and throat.

"No thanks, I don't dance." She made to step to the side, but his hand clamped down on her arm. "I think you do." His tone was terse. "I think you would dance real fine with a body like yours."

"You heard the lady. She does not dance."

He stood behind her assailant, his hand resting on his shoulder. Alara had never heard a voice like it, rich like caramel, deep as the ocean, and smooth. He was at least a head taller than Mr. Oily, and his eyes peered right into hers, seeking her soul, stroking chords, which had not been touched for a decade. With eyes almost as black as his hair, he made her feel like someone of worth, not just a piece of ass in a tight skirt.

But he was definitely not her type.

Oily man's face darkened, his mouth opened, and he swung to see who had him, but his words caught in his throat and he stumbled over them. "I'm...ah, I'm sorry, buddy. Didn't realize she was yours."

"I am certain the lady is her own person, but that gives you no excuse to accost her."

"No. No, of course not. Sorry." The man shifted his gaze and ran a hand over the back of his neck.

"It is not I to whom you should apologize."

"Sorry," he mumbled to Alara before making a hasty retreat into the crowd.

"I could have taken care of myself." Alara raised

her chin as her savior studied her. She came barely to his shoulder.

"I am sure you could." His voice was dark rich chocolate.

He turned in the direction of the table he had occupied, and her hand shot out.

"Wait." She gripped his arm—hard, muscular beneath his coat sleeve.

What was she doing? He was not her type at all, but she knew she didn't want him to leave. Not yet anyway.

"Yes?" He stopped but didn't look back.

"Can I buy you a drink?" She cringed. Did she sound desperate? She saw him stiffen. "In thanks for saving me." She tried to laugh, but it came out more like a squeak.

He turned slowly, and her hand fell away. What were those earlier thoughts? That he was not her sort of man. Was she insane? He was every woman's sort of man. She could feel his body reaching out to her. She had heard of animal magnetism, but... Not even with Ice had she experienced this pull, and she had loved him. Dammit! This was almost palatable, powerful. She had to run. *Put one foot in front of the other and turn away. Run now!*

"One drink?" She forced a smile. "Just to say thank you." How weak could one woman be?

His eyes were dark, brooding. Why didn't he speak? What was he thinking?

"There is no need. I saw you were in trouble. I helped."

"There is every need." What was it about this man that kept her talking, saying things she would never say to another? She was forced to work in a male dominated profession, but always she stood on the outside looking in, never getting close, never wanting to be close. She had loved one man. He had died. Left her—she would not be hurt like that again. She knew she should leave, but… "Please, I insist."

He frowned and glanced away. She thought for a moment he'd refuse.

"Would you sit with me at my table?" he asked, looking back at her.

Alara swallowed hard, mesmerized by his voice—deep, soft, yet strangely compelling, just as his eyes were. Fathomless black eyes that seemed old beyond their years, eyes that seemed to look into her and through her at the same time—as they were now.

"I'll get the drinks," she said too fast. "You do drink, don't you? I noticed that there were no empty glasses on your table." She blushed and glanced into the crowd. She could feel the heat suffusing her cheeks. She had never blushed in her life, and now he would know she had been watching him.

"A red wine will suffice. Do you need help?"

"No…I can manage." Quickly, before he could change his mind, she pushed through the crowd toward the bar. What a fool he must think her, such a naive, inexperienced fool.

She reached the bar and after what seemed forever, finally placed her order. He sat in the shadows again. She caught a glimpse of him as she slowly maneuvered her way back through the room, and although the dance floor was packed, she did not spill a drop. It was as if she was being led safely along and no one could touch her. Like a fly to a spider, but the most irksome part of it was, she was walking into a web of her own making.

****

She was even more beautiful up close—so much like Annabelle. Not exactly, but she was of the same slight build, had the same stubborn tilt to her chin and the same coloring, except Annabelle's hair had grown past her shoulders. And Annabelle had been long ago in another age—an age when things had been simpler, and he had nothing to worry about except the prohibition laws and the local mob.

Already this new technological world was proving more complicated than he had anticipated. Like that card that opened his hotel door. When he awoke this evening, Charlie had been waiting for him, with more of those tubes of blood from the night before. He downed three and his hunger subsided. He stopped seeing Charlie merely as his next meal.

He had asked the boy why he returned. Why had he helped him? Apparently, his young friend still held with the idea that Vincent was going to turn him into a creature of the night. He smiled. Charlie's words, not his. He had no intention of harming the boy. Of making his life a living torture, like his. He enjoyed Charlie's easy charm and quick wit, and he had learned long ago how to control his hunger. Epatha had taught him well. Epatha—teacher, lover, bitch, murderess! He wondered whose life she was ruining now.

Vincent closed his mind to any thought of his maker and remembered back to earlier that evening. Charlie had brought him the clothes he wore, black, how appropriate. Black, for the *black-hearted vamp*, that Charlie had called him when he had insulted the friend the boy had brought to cut his hair. The girl had left in a huff, but she had done a first-rate job.

Gone from society for longer than he could remember, his manners were not as impeccable as they once were. The girl had told him how handsome he appeared with his new haircut and asked if he wished to look in her mirror. He had ordered her out of his room and Charlie had run after the girl, paid her, and reprimanded Vincent for the bad treatment of his friend. He shouted at the boy to go as well but called him back as he'd reached the door. It had been too long since he'd had a friend, and Charlie had helped him. There was no excuse for treating him or the girl in such a detestable way.

Vincent ran his hand through his hair, glorying in the short spiky length beneath his fingers and shifted his gaze from the woman pushing her way through the crowd to the boy on the stage who slashed at his guitar. Hard, heavy, metallic, Charlie's music was not his style. Give him the soft lilting strands of Mozart, any day. Or the orchestras he attended while traveling the world with Epatha.

Epatha! That name again. She had not entered his head in years, yet here she was invading his thoughts on a regular basis.

Was she close? Was she watching him even now?

****

He exuded lethal. A harsh beauty in the dim light. The thought streaked through Alara's mind as she placed the drinks unsteadily on the table, removed her coat, draped it over the back of her chair, and took a seat. She had no idea what she would say to him. Her repertoire of conversations on dates was completely bare and typically uninspiring.

He reached for his glass, took a small sip, sat it back on the table and stared into her eyes.

Nervously, she looked away and downed her margarita in two swallows. "Do you want to get out of here?"

"Where do you suggest we go?"

She swung back. He was laughing at her. He still had the same bland expression, but his tone sounded amused.

"I'm sorry, that must have sounded terribly slutty. I didn't mean it to come out like that. It's just…I don't know why I come here." She glanced at her empty glass, twisting it between her hands.

"Perhaps you were searching for something?" He stood, took her leather jacket from her chair, and waited while she pushed her arms into the sleeves.

"Thanks." She had never been helped on with her coat before, not even by Sam.

The stranger took her arm in his firm grip and a tingling of excitement touched her breasts as he led the way through the crowd. Did the mass seem to part before him, or was it just she'd downed one too many margaritas?

The cold air hit Alara, and she tripped down the step as she exited the door. The stranger caught her arm, but she pulled away.

"Sorry. It appears I've had a little more to drink than I intended." She couldn't look at him. She had made a fool of herself from the moment they'd met. "I'll understand if you call it a night."

He looked down at her, and she could smell his male cologne. It was all that—male, deep, mysterious, with notes of mountain air. He had a way of making her feel soft, vulnerable, a woman.

"Only if you wish it," he returned softly.

"Well, I don't," she blurted, then wished she hadn't.

"Then I shall stay, until you tell me to go." He took her hand and tucked it through his arm. "Now, what shall we do?"

"Actually." She pressed a hand to her temple. "I have a pounding headache."

"Then perhaps I *should* go?" He dropped her arm and pushed his hands into his pockets.

"No, please, don't. That's not what I meant. I thought we could go back to my place."

A dark brow rose, fractionally. "Are you certain that is wise?"

She flushed and looked away. "Now you think I'm forward again."

"Not at all." That amused tone was back.

She studied his face in the dim light. "I thought I could take an aspirin, while you test the red, I received for my twenty-fifth birthday. We could listen to Mozart or Bach. That's if you like classical."

"I like it very much." He took her hand. "Shall we walk?"

"In Seattle at night, on this side of town? I don't think so." She pulled free and stepped out onto the curb as a yellow cab raced around the corner. She gave a shrill whistle and the cab screeched to a halt. After throwing a few short instructions to the driver, she slipped into the rear passenger seat and waited. Her stranger appeared hesitant, and for a moment, she thought he would change his mind, then he slid in beside her.

They barely spoke on the long drive to her apartment in Jackson Place. Her first few questions were answered in monosyllables, and she decided to leave all other conversation until later. She was only chattering nervously, anyway.

The cab drew to a halt, and Alara opened her purse to pay the driver, but her companion leaned forward and handed him several bills. She didn't see how much he gave him, but it must have been generous because the cab driver gave her a wide grin and an enthusiastic thank you before disappearing into the night.

She watched the taillights of the cab vanish, intensely aware of the tall figure standing behind her. What the hell was she doing? She was a cop. A Seattle detective, and she was bringing home a stranger. A man whose name she did not even know, whose name she didn't *want* to know. There was a certain amount of safeness in anonymity.

Perhaps he could be her man for one perfect night, and she would not have to sleep alone in cold sheets for once. If she didn't have to feel, stayed detached, didn't get too close, she could not get hurt. However, first she would have to know she could trust him.

****

Vincent followed the young woman up the concrete steps of her apartment building and stood behind her as she jiggled the key in the lock of the glass security door.

What was he doing here? He crossed his arms over his chest and regarded her in the reflection of the glass. What would he do if she glanced up and took note that his reflection did not fall in behind her? Why was that, he wondered, not for a first time? Was it because he had no soul? Was our reflection really the true face of our soul staring back at us? He shook himself from his mournful thoughts and stared down at the perfect pale arch of the girl's slender neck, beckoning for his attention. His gums tingled from the sweet perfume of her slim young body, singing an age-old tune to him. She was so small, so frail. So easily he could break her. Nonetheless, he knew he wouldn't. Already, his emotions were running deeper than intended. The woman called to him, like a siren's song. Sweet, alluring, her blood would be like honey on his tongue, but the taste of her mouth would be even sweeter, as would the arch of her body against his. He felt a stirring in his loins, kindling a flame in his belly, which he thought long dead with the death of his wife. He knew he should leave, go now, and never see her again. Yet, knew he would not. But he could not help thinking of what happened to people when he got too close. He looked down at her small white hands fiddling with the lock. Those people died.

"Got it." She glanced over her shoulder with a tentative smile. "The lock is old and tends to stick. Sorry 'bout that."

He gave her a strained smile of his own. It was, how did that song go? *Now or never.* She pushed open the door and preceded him inside, and he stepped into the foyer after her.

Swiftly they climbed the two flights of stairs and walked down a narrow hallway. Vincent could have made the journey in a fraction of the time had he swept her into his arms and traveled at his normal pace, but unfortunately that was out of the question.

He counted three doors before she stopped, once

more producing her bunch of keys. They seemed almost too large for her small hand.

"Would you like me to do that?" He reached for the keys.

She handed them to him and moved aside. "I seem all thumbs tonight." She smiled.

He fitted the key to the door, pushed it open, switched on the light around the corner, and allowed her to enter. When he did not follow, she turned, a frown marring her lovely face.

"I thought you were coming in?"

"Do you wish me to?"

"I thought that was understood. You were going to have some wine, listen to Bach." She sounded agitated.

"Then you must ask me."

"I thought... Is this some kind of joke?" She took off her jacket and held it to her chest almost defensively. "If you don't want to come in just say so."

He pushed his hands into his coat pockets and looked into her dark olive-green eyes. He knew she was annoyed, but how could he explain that a vampire could not enter a dwelling unless he was invited. He remained silent, seeing a gambit of emotions cross her face.

"Very well." She sighed. "Would you like to come in?"

He released a heavy breath, stepped into the room, and shut the door behind him. Well, he was here. Now what? A young woman had never invited him home before; this was all new territory.

She tossed her jacket onto the lounge and crossed the carpet to switch on the heating. "Have a seat while I get something for this headache. I'll just be a moment." She disappeared through a door on the left. He heard her rummaging in a drawer in what must have been the kitchen, the clink of a glass, and the running of water.

He had a feeling she was angry with him.

He didn't really care. He could make her forget he ever existed and leave in the blink of an eye, but she interested him, so he would stay awhile. It had been long since he'd shared company with a woman, and she had promised him Bach.

A sleek Siamese sauntered into the living room from what must be a bedroom. At first the animal did not notice him as it stopped to give a luxurious stretch, but on spying him it arched its back, hissed, and bolted back into the bedroom.

A small chuckle escaped his lips. *Astute animals, cats.* Perhaps that is why the Egyptian Pharaohs favored them above all other creatures. They were good at sensing evil. However, he did not like to think of himself as evil—though he knew through the centuries his kind had earned the reputation, with heinous creatures like Epatha on the loose. As for him, he had not killed a soul since being cursed, except for the unfortunate incident in the cabin, and that had been for self-preservation.

He just liked to consider himself a survivor. There were very few of his kind left these days.

Too restless to sit, he moved to a tall window across the room. Pushing aside the red velvet curtains, he peered out onto the bay. A full moon had the whole of the water aglow. Boats of every description dotted the harbor, a bobbing carousel of multicolored lights, and in the distance the faint black shape of the mountains.

He shook his head and ran a hand through his hair.

The scene was far too surreal. By the name of all that was unholy, what was he doing here?

The woman was beautiful, yes, and reminded him far too much of Annabelle, but he had promised himself he would never again get involved with a living being. He had to get out of here!

He pushed away from the window, but too late.

He felt her presence before he heard her. She stood behind him. He could see her reflection, and at the same time realized, he could not see his. He spun too quickly, crashed into her, and caught her in his arms before she fell.

"Forgive me. I never intended to be so clumsy." He guided her so she faced away from the window and led her back to the center of the room.

She pulled free. "Would you like me to take your coat?"

She bit her lip and looked away; she seemed nervous. And she had all reason to be. He was still in two minds as to whether to stay. He should leave right now. He slid his arms from his black leather coat and dropped it onto a nearby armchair, and his mystery woman moved across the room to lift a bottle of wine down from the top shelf of a tall oak wood cabinet. She was so tiny she had to stand on tiptoe to maneuver the bottle.

"Here, let me help." He started to reach up behind her, but she turned.

Too close, pressed to his body in all the right places. He could feel her heart beating into his chest. Her soft, subtle perfume, a mixture of violet and lilac teased his nose and surrounded him, blending with her own womanly scent. He swallowed, fighting his hunger—a different kind of hunger. The hunger a man felt for a woman. The hunger felt for women through every age in history—primeval, earth shattering, eternal.

His fingers threaded through a riot of dark blonde curls as he held her head in place, taking her lips in a deep, drugging kiss that cried for understanding, compassion and she answered him with a fervor that unlocked the dark, cold pit of his heart.

Clothes were no barrier as hands tore at buttons and cloth and found bare flesh. He swept her up and lowered her to the rug, then came down over her in one languid move, bringing with him a promise of completion and one perfect night of passion.

****

Standing by the window, Vincent lifted the curtain and peered out. It was that time between night and dawn when it was still dark, but the first streaks of sunlight would soon mark the horizon. He had to leave to be back at his hotel before sunrise but could not bring himself to move.

She was asleep and had been for some time. They had made love like the world was on the brink of ending, and maybe for him it was true.

He licked his lips, and the thought took him to her bedside. He gazed down at her, bewitched by her beauty, her innocence. She slept on her side, her cheek resting on one arm, her fair hair spread around her head like a bright golden halo. And who was he but the devil, who did not deserve to look upon her face.

Moving slowly, he lifted a lock of hair, twirling it around his finger. So soft, like the woman herself. He let the fine strands trickle through his fingers and unable to help himself, stroked her cheek and slid his fingertips down to the pulse throbbing slow and steady in her throat. Heat rushed through his fingers. Ah, yes, he would have to be careful, incredibly careful. She aroused far more in him than his accursed hunger.

She stirred, and he sank down beside her.

"Sleep, my sweet." He rested his fingertips lightly on her forehead. "Dream of far shores, white knights, and a man who can save you from the demon who lingers at your bedside."

Gently, he bent and stroked her warm salty skin with his tongue. "Rest now, little one, for this night, you have nothing to fear."

She moaned softly as his teeth grazed her throat taking only the smallest amount, tasting only for a moment the sweetest elixir of all. "Sleep, my lovely, 'tis only a dream…"

Chapter Four

Alara opened one eye, then the other, and stretched her arm to feel the bed beside her. With sick disappointment, she realized he was gone—the strange dark man, her midnight lover.

Blood heated her face. She didn't even know his name. What a foolish but wonderful thing to have done. She was a bit worried; they had not used protection, but she'd check with her doctor this afternoon and make certain she had a clean bill of health. The last thing on her mind last night was whether her mystery man was clean or not, but she was certain he'd have to be. It would be nice to have one perfect dream.

She rolled from her bed and almost stumbled as a bout of nausea washed over her. She felt completely zapped of energy. Then again, so would any red-blooded American woman after running a marathon with the stud she'd had in her bed last night. *And the things that man could do with his hands and tongue...*

However, she wouldn't think of that now. Just half a thought had her blushing, and her lack of energy was nothing a good strong coffee couldn't fix. She staggered to the kitchen, set the percolator, and settled on a kitchen chair to wait. As she did so, her gaze drifted to the silver wall clock across the room. Ten a.m.

"What?" Dammit, she was late! Sam would kill

her.

She released a frustrated breath and rested her head against her folded arms on the table, her temples throbbing. Why was her coffee taking so long? She opened one eye and stared accusingly at the percolator.

Fuck. In seven years on the force, she'd never slept in.

She'd forgotten to set her alarm. Sam would be furious or gone without her. Why hadn't he called? She needed her cell phone. She raised her head. Where was it? She'd had it in her purse last night. She stood gingerly, entered the living room, and rummaged in her purse on the gray velvet sofa. She pulled out her cell phone and sank to the carpet. For a moment, she thought she had lost it.

She and Sam were going to check with forensics about the key, and she'd see if they'd finished with the necklace. Annabelle and V...who the heck were they? *Vinny, Valentino, Vince?* Could this person be the lead in solving the case of who killed the McManus boy and the disappearance of the money?

She glanced down at her phone and found it off. She remembered now. She'd switched it off before going to the club. The club—memories of *him* flashed through her mind and she smiled inwardly. *Tall, dark, mysterious, muscles on muscles, my stranger with no name.* She pushed the thought aside. *No time now for dwelling on last night.* She would have the rest of her life for that. She punched in the number that would connect her to Sam. Her head was so thick, she could barely think, and...

"Hello. Detective Grayson."

"Hi, Sam." She pushed a hand through her hair,

uncovering her ear for a clearer reception.

"Is that you, Alara? Where the hell are you?"

"I—"

"I'll rephrase that. All kinds of crap has hit the fan here. Get your skinny ass down to Lincoln Park, now!"

"Yes, boss."

"This is no joking matter, Alara." His tone softened. "Just hurry. I need you. Also, there is something I think you should see."

"Give me fifteen." She hung up, and after two cups of strong coffee and a two-minute shower, she was striding through the green gates of Lincoln Park.

The small memorial park, sectioned off from the public by an iron fence and the police, was a real work in progress. The boys from the South Precinct were already hard at work searching the surrounding flowerbeds, fountain, and trash bins. It appeared they'd called out the whole office on this one.

On the far side of the park near a thatch of high, leafy green bushes, she spied Sam. Beside him lay a body covered in a white sheet.

She made her way toward her partner.

"What's this?"

"I won't ask where you were."

"Don't. I feel like hell warmed over." She bent, drew back the sheet from the body, and was swamped by another bout of nausea. She stumbled and Sam caught her arm, but she pulled away and straightened. It could have been *her* lying there. Her throat mangled, her face white, two small holes torn into the side of her slim neck. The girl was her build, around the same age, fair hair cut in a similar style to Alara's framed her elf-like features. The girl could have been a sister, if she had one.

"Why didn't you warn me?" She glared down at Sam as he dragged the sheet back over the woman.

"I was going to," he said rising. "But you never gave me a chance."

Alara swallowed and glanced away. She had to remain detached and calm, she had to, or she would run from the place screaming. Why was her head still pounding? Surely, she'd had enough coffee. "Who is she?"

"Don't know yet. There's no ID."

"Detective." A police officer spoke at their side. "My men uncovered this in the trash can." The man held out a woman's wallet. Alara slipped on her latex gloves and took the clutch. "Thanks. I'll see this gets back into evidence." She waited for the uniformed officer to walk away, then opened the wallet.

"Susan Williams, from Montlake, age twenty-eight." Her stomach churned again. The girl was the same age as her. "There's over one-hundred dollars in this wallet. It wasn't a robbery." She looked at Sam. "Rape?"

"No." He shook his head. "Nothing points to that, but we'll know more when forensics finishes their examination."

"Time of death?"

"Estimated time, four this morning."

"And the fact that she could be my twin?"

Sam glanced away, clearly uncomfortable. "It could be nothing."

"Or it could be something. Why won't you look at me, Sam?"

He turned back, and she searched his face. Apart

from a slight tenseness about his jaw, his features were devoid of emotion.

She swallowed hard. "Perhaps he thought it was me."

"Who?"

"You know who."

Sam thrust his hands into his pockets and began walking toward the road. "That's ridiculous. This'll be treated as a normal homicide until forensics tells us otherwise."

She hurried up beside him and pulled him around to face her. "You must be joking. You know this was no copycat vampire killing. You know it in your gut, the same way I know it. It's him, and somehow, he knows I'm involved. He must have been watching us at the cabin."

Sam's heavy hands rested on her shoulders. "Now listen to me. This is all circumstantial. The resemblance could be coincidental. Someone might have leaked the story about the boys and the vampire at the cabin. You know how these things work. It only takes one sicko to get wind of it, and here we go again. One such maniac killed your foster mother. Have you forgotten?"

Alara broke free of Sam's hold and her nails bit into her palms. "If I were a man, you would be on the ground by now. I have to live with the knowledge that I couldn't protect her. You don't have to rub it in."

"It wasn't your job," he said, gently, touching her arm.

"I still should've been there. I should've known."

"That may be so, but Ruth's death was no more the work of a vampire than this is."

"And Ice's death. What about that? Was that a

copycat too?"

Sam glanced back at the crime scene, and she watched a muscle twitch in his jaw. His hand dropped to his side. "I didn't say that."

"No, you didn't, but you thought it. And there's still Jimmy's statement about the vampire in the cabin." She stalked past him and headed for her car.

"Alara, wait!"

"What for? You already have the case solved without me."

Sam caught her arm to slow her pace. "Look, I'm sorry, but we won't know the truth, for sure, until forensics is satisfied. We'll check with Fudge Murphy this afternoon and see what he found on the McManus boy." He grinned and released her. "And some good news. A heap of kids playing on the edge of town this morning found Jimmy's backpack.

"Where?"

"On the side of the road, from what I know. One of the kid's mothers called a little after eight."

"Anything in it?"

Sam shrugged. "A few bills of lower denominations. I drove out and picked up the bag myself before the call came in about the girl. The victim's daughter thought there was about twenty thousand in her father's safe the night of the robbery. Unfortunately, there was little left."

Alara shook her head. "Why some people keep so much money on their premises this day and age, I don't know."

"Guess they don't trust banks. Can't really blame them. They don't like me too much."

"Perhaps if you spent a little more on your house

payment, and a lot less on the racetrack, they might regard you in a better light."

Sam gave her a sheepish look. "I didn't know you knew about that."

"Yeah, well I do. The loans officer from the bank called the precinct looking for you. She thought it was your home number. Thought I was your wife. She let off quite a stream before I finally got a word in to explain who I was, and that she'd called your work instead of home."

"Sorry about that. It shouldn't happen again. I had a windfall Saturday, which should about cover the last two payments."

"You won't always win, Sam."

Sam's gray eyes darkened. "I know that," he defended. "But I need to do it. I need to get the house paid off. Only then…" He trailed off, looking into her eyes.

She coughed and stepped back. Sometimes he made her feel uncomfortable. She had a feeling Sam wanted more from her, more than she could give. She respected him too much to ever strap him with her kind of emotional baggage. No, they worked together well. They were partners, and that was the most she had to give to any man.

A dark figure flashed through her mind, but she pushed the image aside. "Anyway," she said, turning back, "that's enough about that. Jimmy will be happy about the recovery of the backpack. The district attorney might be a little more lenient if the forensics can find some fingerprints on it. You know, I almost feel sorry for the kid. Or maybe I'm getting soft."

"You need time off," he said gently. "All this

vampire stuff is taking its toll on you. You need to get away. You must have some leave coming."

"Maybe when this is over."

"It's been a while."

"Five years. I took time off—" She swallowed. "—When Ruth…died."

"Well, you know my opinion."

They continued along the fern-lined path until they reached Alara's Pontiac out front at the curb.

"When are you going to get rid of this heap of—"

"Don't say it. She might hear you." Alara patted her car roof. "She gets me from north to south. Anyway, how could I afford it with the pittance I'm paid?"

"Agreed. I can't fight you on that—I get the same pittance." Sam smiled and watched her climb into the car and fasten her seatbelt. "Talking about south, there's this party tonight. A friend of the captain is throwing him a surprise birthday party. Jenny at reception told me to spread the word. It's at Ross Harbor on the *Fair Maiden*. What do you think?" His smile brightened his craggy handsome features.

"Are you asking me out on a date, Sam?"

Sam laughed softly and clutched his chest. "Do I look like a masochist? I'll leave that to a stronger fool than I."

She released a sigh of relief and clutched at her own heart. "I'm stricken."

He laughed again, but already her thoughts had turned to the dead woman in the park who bore a striking resemblance to herself. She shivered and pushed the thought aside. "Nah, think I'll pass on the party." She forced a smile." I'll send flowers."

"I'm certain he'll love them. Make them red roses so they'll match his nose. But if you change your mind, most of the gang from the precinct will be there. I could give you a lift if you're worried about driving on your own."

"I'll think it over," she said, but knew she wouldn't go. There was no way she could face another night on the town with the drums that were playing in her head. "I'll see you at the precinct. Actually, why don't you jump in with me and get one of the guys to bring your car back?"

"Nah, I've a few leads I want to check. Give me a half hour." Sam was about to turn away, but abruptly swung back. "Why don't you look in on Fudge? He might have something on the key that we could work with."

"Good idea. See you at the lab." Alara closed her window, blocking out the cold air and the noise of the Seattle traffic, and watched Sam stride down the path toward his car. Then she lowered her head onto her folded arms across the steering wheel and sighed. So much had happened in so short a space of time—the death of the boy in the cabin, Jimmy's story of a vampire, the dead girl with the uncanny resemblance to herself, the recovered backpack, the key, the necklace.

She was so close. She raised her head and thumped her fist on the steering wheel. This time she would get the bastard. She could feel it in her veins. This time she would get Ice's murderer, and when she did, she would make him wish he had stayed in hell.

Chapter Five

At sunset that evening, Charlie let himself into Vincent's hotel room. Making no attempt at silence, he marched over to the bed and switched on the bedside lamp. He swore on finding the bed empty, and stiffened at the sound of a deep, cultured voice behind him.

"You were looking for me?"

The hairs on Charlie's nape prickled. He drew a deep breath, straightened, and turned.

Vincent stood drying his thick black hair, a second towel knotted low on his hips. He looked like any ordinary guy getting ready for a date, but Charlie knew better. He'd seen this man down three or four tubes of blood in one sitting. No human could do that. No, Vincent might look like an ordinary bloke, but looks were known to be deceiving.

"Did you do this?" He slapped the newspaper he carried down on the small meal table.

The headline read—*Vampire! Young woman found in Lincoln Park, drained of blood.*

Vincent dried the water from the back of his neck, pinning Charlie with his gaze. "Do you think I did it?"

Charlie picked up the backpack he'd dropped on entering and strode to the bar fridge, pulled a can of beer from inside the fridge door, cracked it, and downed a couple of gulps. "Don't know," he said, after a loud belch. "I saw you leave with that chick last night from the club. You didn't come back here. I waited till four. Plus, the girl answers the description of the dead woman." He slid a sideways look at Vincent and watched him snatch up the *Times*. For several minutes the vampire scanned the article, then cursing loudly tossed it onto the bed. If he could have gone any paler, Charlie swore he just had.

"Well, did you?"

"Did I what?

"Kill her."

"Of course, I didn't kill her. I'm not a cold-blooded murderer." Vincent dropped the towel, snatched the black jeans from the end of the bed, and dragged them up over his hips. "However, I have a good idea who did."

"You mean there's two of you?"

"There are a lot more than two, but we usually do not draw attention to ourselves."

Charlie gulped. "More than two?" He peered into the shadows, and Vincent smiled. A sight Charlie hadn't seen before. It vanquished the severity from his face, making him look younger, yet somehow more chilling.

"I very much doubt they are in Seattle. They like New York better. More people. They can blend in."

"You've been to New York?"

"Not for forty years."

"Forty years, that would make you how old?"

Vincent shook his head, settled onto the bed, and pulled on his black socks. "If I told you, you would not believe me."

"Try me. There's a show on television about a vampire who is two hundred years old. You can't be that old."

He looked up and raised his brow. "I was born in Venice in the year 1771. Does that answer your question?"

"Wow." Charlie rolled his eyes. "It's true. Vampires do live forever. How cool."

"If they are not decapitated, tied up out in the sun, stabbed through the heart with a silver or wooden stake, or shot with a silver bullet," Vincent replied evenly. "Then yes, it might be possible. The oldest I ever met was an Egyptian noble born 1210 BC in the last few years of *Tuthmosis III.*"

"Wow." Charlie released a heavy breath and began packing the blood he'd filched from the blood bank into the fridge. "I don't know how much more of this I'll be able to get." He tossed one of the tubes to Vincent. "I almost got caught tonight, and Kate found her keys missing when I forgot to put them back on the hook. She asked what I wanted with them."

Vincent ripped the top off the blood tube, downed the contents in several long swallows, and dropped the empty plastic packet into the black bag that lined the small bin beside his bed. He caught the next tube Charlie threw his way, repeated the procedure, and wiped the towel across his mouth, leaving a red stain.

"I will deal with that when the time comes. There are always ways."

Charlie frowned. "How? What ways?" A shiver flickered down his spine, and his nape tingled.

Vincent gave him a steady look. "You have no need to fear me, Charlie. I do not make a habit of snacking on people who help me."

"That's not what you said that first night."

"I was angry, tired, and I stank like a cornered skunk. I wanted to be rid of you."

"Next time just tell me to piss off."

"I will do that. I have been out of polite society for way too long. My social graces are not what they once were."

"They didn't look too rusty last night when you picked that girl up."

The boy raised a brow in question, and Vincent gave what could almost have passed for another smile but refrained from commenting. Instead, he grabbed a clean black T-shirt from the armchair closest to him and pulled it over his head.

"This lot of blood should keep for a couple of days. Just make sure when you leave tonight, you remind the desk clerk that I will not be requiring room service."

"Sure." Charlie finished packing the last eight tubes into the fridge and gently closed the door. "It might look a bit weird if they open the refrigerator to stock up the mini bar and find it full of blood packs. Though you better let the maids clean the room at least once a week, or they might get suspicious."

"The refrigerator will be empty by Friday. Why don't you tell them to send someone up then? Make it worth their while."

"Ah, that's another problem. The money you gave me is all gone."

He raised a brow. "So soon?"

Charlie shrugged and spread his hands. "What can I say? The cost of living has skyrocketed since you last surfaced. This hotel alone costs the earth...and the clothes." He saw Vincent's fist close over a key attached to the thin gold chain he wore around his neck.

He frowned, then fumbled with the catch on the chain. When it refused to give, he yanked it from his neck, and sank onto the bed, looking down at the chain hanging loosely from his fingers. "It's gone. Of all the idiotic…I just thought…I never checked…it must still be in the cabin."

"Cabin? You're not making sense. What cabin? What did you lose?"

Vincent lowered his hands and rose. "Nothing. Well, it was something—another key, but it is of no consequence. It was of sentimental value only." He unhooked the key from the chain and passed it to Charlie. "You will travel to New York. I have a safety deposit box in the New York City Bank. Empty out the contents and bring it back to me. Understand?"

Charlie tucked the key into his pocket. "Of course." He grinned. "You can trust me."

"I know that." Vincent smiled coldly, and Charlie swallowed. "Because there is no place you can hide that I could not find you."

"There was no need to say that." Charlie's lips thinned. "I thought we were friends, and friends watch each other's backs."

He pushed to his feet. "Forgive me, and you are right, but as we have already established, my manners are somewhat lacking. Many years have passed since I called anyone, friend."

Charlie sighed. "Forget it." He stood and wandered to the window to peer out into the darkening night. "Do you think it *was* the girl you met last night that was murdered in the park?" He spun and pinned Vincent with his gaze. "Who was she anyway?"

"Unfortunately, the young lady and I did not

exchange names. But no, it is not Epatha's way. It was a warning. She would have chosen someone that looked like the young woman I was with. That is how it begins."

"What do you mean begins?"

"She has done this before."

"Epatha. Is that 'er name? Weird."

"She is the Egyptian noble of which I spoke. Rich beyond description, and powerful, but unfortunately, she fell for the wrong man."

Charlie scooped up the black garbage bag from the bin, knotted it, and stuffed it into his backpack. "And you know her, how?"

"She sired me."

The boy let out a soft whistle. "You were the wrong man?"

"No, she killed the *wrong man* after he betrayed her. I was her plaything."

"Then why is she threatening you?"

"I left her, and no one leaves Epatha, unless Epatha wills it. She is not after me. She could not make me suffer enough. She wants the woman I was with last night. Or, she will be, unless I stay away from her. She kills any woman I get close to."

Charlie flopped down into the armchair by the fireplace. "Nice lady."

"If you like psychopathic vampire women."

"I thought—" Charlie looked away. "I thought, seeing as you were a male vampire, that you would be stronger, faster. That you would have the advantage?"

"Had she been a normal vampiress that would be the case, but Epatha was made by the Egyptian High Priest Imohn-Atra, who devoted his life to the study of

Anubis, the God of the Dead. Apparently, he unearthed an ancient Egyptian scroll pertaining to immortality, but when he translated the script, he messed up the wording and it backfired, transforming him into a very powerful vampire. He got his immortality all right, but he needed blood to sustain it. Epatha, being his lover, was also his first victim, and he passed onto her some of his power."

"Power? What power?"

"She has the ability to shapeshift into a hawk, and mist, and if she keeps to the shadows, she can move about in daylight, but not only that, Imohn-Atra had a magical red stone in his possession. The stone was thought to have been taken from the treasure trove of Anubis. It rendered the wearer immortal. He was unable to die. She betrayed the High Priest by stealing the stone and killing him. She wears the stone about her neck at all times, and on both occasions I have attempted to track her down and kill her, she has escaped by using the power of the stone. You see, it glows blood red when another vampire is in close proximity."

"You could turn me. I could help you take her down."

"Thanks, Charlie, but she would eat you for breakfast. And we've had this talk about me siring you before. I will not do it. I like you too much to wish a living death upon you."

"Shouldn't that be my decision?" Charlie's fist clenched. He wanted it so much.

"Not if I can help it."

Charlie sprang to his feet and threw up his hands. He opened his mouth to speak, shut it, then tried again. "It's not fair. It'd be so great."

Vincent slammed his fist into his palm. "You know nothing about that of which you speak. You are a gullible fool." He stalked to the window, dragging aside the drapes to stare out at an unforgiving sky. Raindrops clawed at the glass, as the weather turned nasty. "You will never again stand on a hill and watch the sunset, feel a sunrise touch your face, or wriggle your toes in the warm sand on a beach. You will see everyone you love wither and die, if you do not kill them in your first initial blood lust. When you are turned you have no control, and unrestrained or urged on, it can lead to the death of people you love."

"But it wasn't like that for you."

"Was it not?" Vincent turned on Charlie, his pale face etched in harsh lines. "Do you forget Epatha was my instructor in the ways of the undead? My father dropped to his knees and prayed to the almighty for my forgiveness as I ripped out his throat. His blood still stains my hands." He stared down at his fingers as if still seeing the crimson liquid marks. "I will never forget the taste of his blood on my lips. And my little sister…it was the night after her coming out ball. She looked at me with such trust in her eyes, even as she saw me rise up like a foul demon from our father's body." His voice broke. "The memories of those first days… They never leave you."

Charlie's voice softened. "This Epatha, she must be some queen bitch, huh?"

"The Emperess of all bitches and more." Vincent sank onto the bed, staring down blankly at his clenched fists. When he glanced up, he'd wiped all expression from his face, but there was a hint of steel in his voice. "She killed the only woman I ever loved and set it up to look like I had committed the crime."

****

Later that night, Vincent stood outside the woman's door. At first, he told himself he'd wanted to make sure she was all right, that he'd been mistaken about the newspaper article. He had satisfied that curiosity the moment he had stopped outside room fourteen. He could hear her heart beating on the other side of the door. Sense the soft notes of her rose perfume. Hear each breath expelled from her lungs and the soft murmur of her voice as she spoke to her cat.

He knew he should leave, never to see her again. If he stayed, he would be putting her in danger from Epatha's insane jealousy. Nevertheless, he needed to stay. Needed to hear the soft lilt of her voice, feel her touch on his skin, her heart race beneath his hands. Taste the sweetness of her mouth, and her blood. No. Not her blood, never again her blood. The first taste had been too heady, like sweet wine.

The door swung open, and her eyes widened at the sight of him. She was lovely. A short royal blue cocktail gown clung in all the right places, and over her arm, she carried a black beaded shawl and small matching handbag. Her cropped blonde hair curled artfully across her forehead and around her shell-like ears, giving her delicate pointed face a gamin look.

"I was about to knock." He spoke softly.

"I...I wasn't expecting you." She reached up to push her hair from her eyes. "I was going out."

"Perhaps another night, then." He stepped out of her way and started to turn, but her hand shot out.

"Wait." She hesitated and her hand lowered to her side as he glanced down at it. "Actually, I was heading to the marina. There's a party…" She peered down the dimly lit hallway, then back at him. "Would you like to join me?"

"A party?" The words gave him pause. Long years had passed since he had enjoyed anything resembling a party. He and Annabelle had attended a few dances in the forties, but that had been long ago. Times were different. Music had a different beat. He looked down at his black turtleneck sweater and jeans. "I am not dressed for anything formal."

"It's nothing too formal. A surprise party for my boss, that's all."

"You did not say what you did for a living."

She smiled sweetly. "That makes two of us."

He searched her face, then held out his arm. "So, it does. Shall we go?"

She stepped over the threshold, locked the door, and linked her arm through his.

****

Ross Harbor was aglow and the party in full swing when they made their way up the ramp to the *Fair Maiden*. The ship, ablaze with lights, reverberated with the crooning tone of Frank Sinatra, Chief Hendrick's favorite song master.

No sooner had she stepped on board than Alara heard her name called and spun to find Sam striding toward them.

"I see you made it." He smiled. "And managed to bring a friend." He raised a sandy-colored brow at her and held out his hand to Vincent. "I'm Sam Grayson, Alara's partner.

He shook Sam's hand with a firm grip. "Vincent," he returned without elaborating. "Partner?" He glanced quizzically at Alara.

She threw him an innocent smile.

Sam waited, and when there was no last name forthcoming, he dropped Vincent's hand and turned to Alara.

"Forensics called. They've pinned down the origin of the key." He grinned. "We'll talk later, or better still, tomorrow. It's party time!" He beckoned a waiter bearing a tray of champagne, snatched up a glass, and waited for Vincent and Alara to help themselves to a wine, then he gave Vincent a hearty slap on the back, almost spilling his drink. "Look after this girl," he said in a dramatic stern tone, "or you will have to deal with me." With a soft glance at Alara he turned and pushed his way through the crowd."

"So, Vincent." Alara raised a brow. "That was Sam, and I guess from what he said, you have gathered I'm a detective."

He ignored her words. "Alara. Such a pretty name. Sounds old worldly."

"My mother's." She glanced over the side of the ship into the burnished water, and he watched her for a moment sensing she didn't want to talk about her family. He offered his hand. "Shall we take a stroll on the top deck?" The view might be quite lovely, but he was not looking at the water; he was looking at her.

She lowered her lashes. "I'd enjoy that, yes."

Alara led the way through the party revelers— women dressed in everything from finery and diamonds to short, outlandish miniskirts with shimmering tops, and men with tuxedoes or jeans and Tee's. It seemed the boss's party was turning out to be everyone's party. She noted her friend Sarah through the crowd at the bar with her fiancé, Randy, and raised her hand in a wave. The redhead arched a brow in question, but Alara shook her head, raised a hand in greeting and kept walking. They climbed the steps to the observation deck in silence, pushing past several merrymakers to come to a halt at the bow of the ship. The air was full of salt with a slight hint of fish and just a touch of rain, which had decided to stay at bay. The marina was alive with dancing lights on the water, and the windows of the houses in the distance provided an enchanting, illuminated backdrop.

Alara leaned on the railing, her champagne glass clasped tightly between her hands, and cast Vincent a shy glance. He seemed so calm, so cool, like something out of an ageless cigarette advertisement. She was totally out of her league. She looked back down at her glass and twirled it in her hand. "So, what next?"

He set his drink on the deck beside him and took the glass from her shaking fingers and lowered it next to his. Then he brought her hand to his lips. "This will go only as far as you wish it to go."

"And if I wish it to go further," she asked softly.

"Then we will take one day at a time."

****

Her lips were warm and pliant against his, and bittersweet from the champagne. Vincent wished only to crush her to his chest, sweep her up, and transport her to her apartment to taste again the heady rapture of her body. However, he held himself at bay, as he held back the blood lust that raged within. She was so vulnerable, so small in his arms. He wished only to protect her. Pushing her to arm's length he picked up their glasses and handed hers back.

"So, I suppose it is now that all the awkward questions must start," he stated, staring into the night.

She laughed softly. "I suppose so. Or we could just play pretend again."

He turned and studied her face. "Is that what you want, Alara?"

The look she gave him was open, vulnerable. "I could say yes?"

He cupped her jaw. "That way you would not have to relive the pain?"

She pulled away and stared down at the water. "Am I that transparent?"

"It is in your eyes, but you do not have to tell me."

"Yes." She gave him a sideways glance. "I do. I've kept it bottled up too long." She heaved a sigh and began to speak, quietly at first, then her voice gained momentum. "My full name is Alara Jane Gale. Detective Alara Gale." She smiled at him quickly then returned her gaze to the water. "Brief past—I was born in Sydney, Australia. My parents and brother died in a plane crash when I was eleven. Having no relatives in Australia, I was shipped off to live with my mother's sister, my only relative who promptly died a year later of a lingering illness. Placed with a foster family, I was raised by a foster father who liked nothing more than getting drunk every Friday and using me as a punching bag.

"I hit the streets when I was fifteen, where I joined a street gang and met up with a boy called Ice. We lived together for a short time." She gave him a quick glance. "Until Ice was shot performing a robbery. A policewoman named Ruth Robins took pity on me. She'd never married and had no children. It was she who encouraged me to go back to high school and finish it."

Vincent saw her swallow. "Ruth was killed by a serial killer two years later. You could say I originally joined the force to find her killer, but that was in the beginning." She drew back from the rail and turned to face him. "I love my job. I love the people I work with, and I wouldn't give it up for anyone. Not at least till…" She straightened. "So that's me." She raised her chin. "Take it or leave it."

So defiant, so afraid of rejection, frightened of being hurt. Vincent cupped her chin. Smooth and warm beneath his fingers. He could feel nothing but compassion for her. She'd been through so much, and still he would put her through more. What could he say to this beautiful fragile woman? What could he offer? What could he give but hurt?"

"Now it's your turn," Alara said, her smile too brittle.

He pushed his hands into his pockets. "My turn?" He frowned.

"It's only fair." She cocked her head to the side, in that little girl's way she had, and his black heart melted all over again. Feathers and iron this woman, pain and pleasure. She could very well be the death of him, if he fell too deeply, if he got too involved. He should step back, walk out of her life, but he knew he would not. And she was a policewoman. What in the name of— what was he getting himself into? Sam had mentioned a key. Was it just coincidence? Or was it his key? Had these two been in his old cabin?

He looked down into her dark-green eyes trying to read her mind, but unfortunately that gift had been lost to him when the witchdoctor had laid his curse.

Vincent released her and leaned back against the ship rail. What could he tell Alara, which was not too much and not too little, that would not sound suspicious? He laughed inwardly. That he was a son of a nobleman, almost two hundred and ten years old, instinctive, patient, self-disciplined? Traits he'd developed to survive. That he'd massacred his whole household, including his fifteen-year-old sister and a loving father after being turned to vampirism, and as a special gift, he could shape-shift into a wolf, and turn to mist? He laughed softly beneath his breath. Oh yes, and he had no reflection and was almost immortal. He released a heavy sigh. "I am twenty-nine." He spoke at last, his words cutting into the silence as he wished for a time that would never be again. He swallowed. "I was born in Venice, at sunrise." He stared down into the sea. "My mother used to tell the story of how she stared out the window and the whole of the channel glowed blood red as I broke from her body." He shivered. "My family is dead."

Alara covered his hand with hers. "I'm, sorry. If it's too painful—"

"It was long ago." There was a wistful note in his voice, which he disguised with a cough. He was about to speak again, but he glanced over Alara's shoulder, right into the exquisite, smug face of Epatha.

Standing about twenty feet away, dressed in a long ruby sheath, a scarlet jewel sparkling at her throat, blue-black hair piled atop her head. She appeared no older than the first evening he had met her at Covent Garden—the night she had sired him. A shiver washed down his back.

She sashayed her way toward the stairs, and he frowned and downed his last mouthful of champagne.

Alara turned, then looked back at Vincent with a mixture of curiosity and sadness.

"Do you know that woman?"

She had obviously followed his gaze.

"An old friend with whom I must speak."

He saw her swallow and the light go from her eyes. "Of course." She stepped back. "Don't let me stop you." Her tone was hard.

"It is not like that." He reached for her chin and turned her to face him. "I would like for you to wait here. Will you do that?" He pressed her hand between his and gazed into her eyes. "Will you promise me you will not leave, no matter how long I am gone?"

She frowned. "What is it? Has that woman got some kind of hold over you? Is she threatening you?" She gripped his wrist and held his gaze. "I am a detective, remember. If she's making a nuisance of herself—"

"No," he lied, forcing a smile. "It is not like that. As I said, an old friend, that is all. Now, I must go before she leaves." He extracted himself from her grip and backed away. "Remember, wait here, or better still, find your friend Sam and stay with him." He turned and ran in the direction Epatha had vanished.

****

Vincent needn't travel far before he found the one he sought. Epatha was waiting on the dock below the gangplank in full view of the party. Clever witch, he thought. She knew she would be safe within sight of the ship.

"Vincent, darling." Her smile was cloyingly sweet

as she reached to take his hands. The pendant at her neck glowed bright red, signifying his presence. "I see you have another charming little friend. Do you never tire of this game?" She lowered her hands when he refused to touch her, and her tone hardened. "I see you have not changed your mind." She laughed softly. "But mark my words. You are *mine*. You will always be *mine*. You can play your little games as much as you like, but I made you. You promised in blood. Mine for eternity, you vowed. I have not forgotten. I will *never* forget." She ran her red-tipped fingers down his arm and her tone softened. "Do you not remember, Vincent, how good we were together? I miss you. I am lonely. You were my other half. Part of me. *Please*." Her hand tightened. "I have never begged for anything in my life, but I need you. Don't you reminisce of how we traveled the world, and the world fell at our feet? There was nothing we could not have, not do. We lived like gods."

"I *remember*." He almost spat the words as he stepped back from her touch. "The trail of blood you weaved, the fear in the eyes of the populace, your laughter as your victims pleaded for their lives. And yes, I am ashamed to say for a while I enjoyed it, was part of it, but when you swept through that orphanage in France after the war, that finished me. The eyes of the children still haunt my sleep. No more will I be part of your deranged world. Do you think I would touch you again after Annabelle?"

"Annabelle." The name exploded from her tongue. "That insipid little tramp! What sweet revenge it was ripping out her throat. Her blood was the elixir that kept me going over these years."

"You demon bitch—" He lurched and grasped her

by the throat, squeezing hard, yet even so, she smiled.

"You know you cannot kill me like this," she whispered tightly, "and you are putting on a show for your friends aboard ship."

He glanced up to see a small crowd peering over the side of the docked ship. Reluctantly he released her and smiled tightly, giving her a brief bow. "I *will* kill you one day. Make no mistake."

She ignored his words and slowly stroked her throat, trailing her long slender fingers down her décolletage to the tip of her breast. "You always were so volatile, kept me on my toes. Not like those other simpering wimps I sired. You were the only one among them who heated my blood—who had balls. That reminds me." She raised a delicate arched brow. "Did you receive my message?"

He frowned and dragged his gaze from the finger encircling her nipple and stared over her shoulder into the bay. "What message?"

"The girl in the park of course."

His jaw hardened. "You touch one hair on Alara's head."

"So, that is her name." She smiled again, coldly. "You need only to come back to me."

"When a blizzard freezes hell."

She stepped back into the shadows. "Then, let the games begin." In a blink she was gone.

Vincent had never seen a vampire move as fast as Epatha—another reason he had been unable to kill her. He was fast, but not that fast.

He glanced up at the ship. Not a soul had been watching.

****

Alara was gone. He searched the deck where he left her, but she was nowhere. He sought her friend Sam, and found Alara had left over a quarter of an hour ago.

Vincent's stomach churned. Was Epatha, even now, exacting her revenge on Alara?

He had to stay calm until he disembarked the ship. He thanked Sam for his help and hurried toward the gangplank. As he did so, a woman called his name.

He spun and watched as she sauntered toward him. The girl was around Alara's age with layered auburn hair and dressed in a skintight silver gown.

"Sorry," she gushed, "I could not help noticing you were with Alara earlier this evening." She looked away, then back at him. When he didn't speak, she went on. "I hope everything is all right between you two. Alara does not usually date...and...I don't want to see her hurt."

"As I do not. Can you tell me, did you see her leave?"

Her voice rose in surprise, and her expression darkened. "Well, yes, that is why I am speaking to you. Alara was with a woman in a red evening dress. I thought it odd that she should arrive with you and be leaving with a woman."

Vincent gripped her arm. "How long ago? This lady, did she have black hair? Did Alara appear upset?"

"Ouch! No." The young woman wrenched free and rubbed at her upper arm. "Alara was laughing. It was about fifteen minutes ago, and they were walking along the pier toward the parking lot." She rubbed her offended arm again and threw him an accusing look.

"Thank you, and sorry if I hurt you." He glanced at

the wharf and shifted uncomfortably. "I did not mean to manhandle you. I am worried about Alara." He backed away. "I must go." He turned and fled down the ramp.

"I hope you find her and make up," the woman called after him.

"That makes two of us."

He hit the darkness and blended at warp speed with the night.

****

Vincent's essence took form within Alara's bedroom. The Siamese sleeping upon her pillow sprang awake, glared at him with flaming blue eyes, hissed, and shot off into the living room. Alara was obviously not in her room.

He had searched half the city, cafés, bars, and bistros. Even in wolf form he had been unable to pick up her scent. He couldn't begin to guess where Epatha had taken her.

Tired, defeated, he had taken sustenance from an old vagrant on the east end of town. The man would never remember. Then he traveled here to make certain Alara had not returned home. Deep down he knew her apartment would be empty.

He moved from one object to another touching, fingering that which was hers, gaining a sense of who and what she was. The room told nothing of her life. She owned little in the way of trifles. The only concession to femininity was a floral overstuffed chair in the corner, the piece of furniture totally out of place amid its dark masculine counterparts.

Vincent shifted to the dressing table, thankful for the night's shadows as he stood before a mirror that would bear him no reflection. About to turn away, something sparkling in the moonlight caught his attention. He reached for the gold locket on the dresser with a mixture of familiarity and dread. It was Annabelle's—his. How did Alara get it? The cabin? She could only have found the locket in the cabin. He wondered what else she knew. Or, what else she *would* know once she discovered the mystery of the key and what it unlocked? He wiped the locket clean on his sweater and dropped it back onto the dresser.

He knew he should steal the necklace, but beside it sat a small brown paper bag, like a forensics bag, and the chain had been tagged. He didn't have the heart to let Alara take the blame for a piece of tagged evidence lost while in her possession. However, it would probably be a moot point if Epatha had already taken Alara's life.

Turning to mist and exiting the way he entered, he materialized on the street below and disappeared into the shadows to continue his search. He would return this way later.

****

Alara fumbled with her key, pushed open the door, and switched on the light. She jumped as a dark figure loomed over her.

"Where have you been?"

Alara clutched her chest still getting over the initial shock of finding Vincent in her apartment. However, her shock turned to anger. What right did he have to invade her privacy? She had only met the man twice.

"How did you get in?" she asked, a chill to her voice.

"You did not answer my question."

She dodged around him, moved to dump her

evening bag on the couch, and flopped down beside it. "I've been with your sister. We had coffee, then moved onto clubbing." She tried to lighten her tone. "She knows the most incredible haunts."

Vincent frowned. "Sister?"

"Epatha." Her response held a hint of impatience. "She told me of your quarrel, and I agree with her. I think it's time you let go and move on."

He raised a brow. "You do, do you. What exactly did she tell you, and why did you not wait for me?"

"Epatha said you were called away on business. She asked me out for coffee. I couldn't really refuse as she *is* your sister. And I enjoyed myself. She's really quite fabulous."

"You are not to see her again."

"Really." It was her turn to raise a brow and she came to her feet. "Why not? What the hell is this all about, Vincent? You can't keep a grudge forever, surely. From what Epatha told me, she has already apologized a dozen times. Build a bridge and get over it." She made to push past him. She needed coffee, but he grasped her arm.

"You are not to see her again. Did you not hear me?"

She stared down at his hand on her arm. "What *is* your problem? I'm a grown woman. I can see who I damn well please. And let me go."

He released her and crossed his arms. "What did she tell you?"

She flopped back in her seat and looked away. "That you were accused of murdering your wife, Annabelle, and there was a time after you were arrested that Epatha believed you had really done it. However, when you were acquitted, she realized what a tragic mistake she had made." She peered up at his hard expression. "She really is sorry. She wants to make it up to you."

Vincent gave a half laugh. "I bet she does." He turned and strode to the window. "You know nothing about the matter. The woman is a treacherous, conniving bitch." He spun and thumped the coffee table. "She is dangerous. You will not see her again."

"Oh, won't I?" Alara came to her feet. "I've had enough of this. Get out." She'd found Epatha nothing but charming, and she would not stand here and listen to her character being maligned. She strode to the door and yanked it open. "Don't come here again." She crossed her arms as she waited for him to move. "I will not be told what to do by any man, especially in my own apartment." She pointed at the hallway. "Just go, please, I don't want you here."

"I was invited," Vincent murmured, heading for the door, but before he stepped through, he stopped. "Just do not let her in, or be alone with her, promise me that."

She shook her head. "I will promise you nothing. I do not even know who you are any more. If I ever did. How do I know you did not murder your wife? From what Epatha said they never found her killer."

Vincent turned and the look on his pale face was lethal. "Because I loved that woman beyond life itself. Had I been able to give her my soul, I would have." He stepped through the door and shut it quietly behind him.

Chapter Six

Alara was tired, hungry, and her head thumped as if a jackhammer resided in her skull. In the gloomy hallway, she fumbled with her key, and fit it to the lock. Easing open the door, she fully expected to see Vincent, but when she flicked on the light the room was empty. Dealing with her initial disappointment, she was brought from her sad reverie by Jesse winding affectionately in and around about her legs.

With a small half laugh and a murmured greeting to her furry friend, she hitched her handbag over her shoulder and reached down to pet her cat. At least someone loved her. She sighed heavily and hugged Jesse to her chest. The cat struggled and she had to release her.

Her thoughts drifted back to last night. When Vincent had stepped through the door, he'd closed it quietly behind him.

Too quiet. It would have been better had he slammed it.

She listened for his footsteps, but they didn't come. She ran to the door, pulled it open, and called his name, but he was gone. The silence of a dimly lit hallway glared back at her. She shut the door and sank to the floor, covering her face with her hands. What had she done, but allowed her temper to get the better of her? Something she had not done in years. She couldn't take back her hateful words. It was too late, and she did not even know where he lived, or how to find him.

She strode into the kitchen, dumped her handbag onto her small pinewood table, and moved to fix a well-earned cup of espresso. Although she had told him not to come there, she missed him. She knew she had only met him twice, but it seemed like she'd always known him. Her mistake was in letting him get close. Then, she had let her tiredness and anger get the better of her, and now she was paying the price in loneliness. It was her own stupid fault.

She rummaged in the kitchen drawer for two aspirin and downed the pills with a glass of water. After feeding Jesse and brewing her coffee, she sank onto a wooden chair with her cup cradled between both hands.

After downing several cups of coffee at the station, she'd looked forward to coffee that actually tasted like coffee, and not dirty dishwater, bitter and foul. Or was that her job? She hadn't thought she would ever tire of detective work, but lately it had become a drain.

Like tonight.

It was nine thirty. She had started work at the crack of dawn, when Sam had called with a lead pertaining to a homicide they had been working on for four months. It took until noon to locate the perpetrator in question and at eight p.m. they finally wrung a confession from her.

A knock sounded at the door and Alara swore softly. Who the hell would be knocking on her door at ten p.m.?

A face of a man with black hair and dark mesmerizing eyes flashed before her, but she pushed it aside and rose.

Trudging across the carpet she slid aside the shutter and peeped out. It was not Vincent. She sensed another twinge of disappointment and tried to swallow the lump lingering in her throat, cursing that his image would not dispel.

It was Epatha, sheathed in a hip hugging black skirt, sheer ebony stockings, stylish white designer top, and a Gucci handbag looped over her arm. She was the epitome of fashion.

Alara unlatched the door with a frown that quickly turned to a smile. "Epatha, how great to see you, but I really wasn't expecting you."

"I know, but we had such a marvelous time last evening, I wondered if you were up for a repeat performance. I did drop by earlier, but you were nowhere about."

Alara pushed a hand through her mop of unruly curls. "I was late leaving the station."

"Long day?"

She released an exaggerated sigh. "Exhausting."

"So, no night out?" The bright note dropped from Epatha's voice.

Alara pulled a sad face. "Not tonight, sorry, but we will do it again. Promise."

"Perhaps I could join you for coffee?" The dark-haired woman raised a finely arched brow and gave a saccharine smile.

She started to step forward, but Alara blocked her path, returning her smile smoothly, betraying nothing of her annoyance, when she really wanted to tell her to go. What was it about this woman that bothered her tonight? Was it her too bright personality? Her insistent manner? Or the way she had almost knocked her out of the way in an attempt to get into her apartment? Alara had enjoyed their outing last night, but tonight something did not quite gel.

Could it be Vincent's parting words echoing in her mind, *"The woman is a treacherous conniving bitch. She is dangerous. Don't let her in."* Alara shook her head. "Sorry, perhaps another time. I'm tired and I have an early start in the morning. Maybe next week." She reached into her back pocket, pulled out a leather card wallet and handed Epatha her private card. "Call me. I know a great little spot off the back of Fifth Street."

Epatha took the card and dropped it into her handbag. "It's a date. Next week, then." She leaned forward, dropped a swift kiss on Alara's cheek just as Jerry, Alara's neighbor, stepped from his apartment. He called a greeting to Alara as Epatha spun to leave.

"Wait." She called Epatha back.

"Yes." The dark-haired woman turned.

"I was wondering…if you might have Vincent's phone number, or address? I need to contact him."

All expression dropped from Epatha's face to be replaced by a spark of some indefinable emotion in her bright turquoise eyes. "No. I am sorry I do not. As I told you last night, it has been long since my brother and I spoke. However, if you do come by the information, I would much appreciate it if you shared. He and I still have much to discuss." She glanced down at her sparkling, diamond wristwatch. "Now, I really must go. I remembered I do have another appointment after all." She raised her hand in an exaggerated wave and disappeared along the corridor.

****

Epatha ran halfway down the first flight of stairs,

then vaporized and materialized to lean on the front door jam, cursing into the darkness.

Alara may have escaped her this time, but next time she would not be so lucky.

She had planned the evening so well. They were to visit a nice cozy bar, and she would pump Alara for all she knew about Vincent. It would have looked too suspicious last night. Then they would leave together, and Epatha would drink her dry and leave her in the alley behind the club. Vincent would read of the murder in the paper and be heartbroken all over again. Eventually, he would realize he had no option but to return to her.

However, Alara, the little trollop had ruined her plans. Too tired indeed! She had not even invited her into her apartment. What had that been about? Had Vincent warned her? Surely not. There was no way he would have told Alara she was a vampire. For to do so, he would have to expose his own secret.

Footsteps on the stairs dragged her from her thoughts. She slid the pins from her hair and shook her wild black locks down around her shoulders. She flicked open the top button of her blouse as the young man who had emerged from the apartment next door to Alara's came into view.

She smiled and moved from the shadowy doorway.

The man drew closer then frowned as her face became clear. He peered back up the stairs. "Didn't…didn't I see you upstairs in the hallway?

Epatha dropped a heavy sigh. "My twin sister, Lilly. She really is a pain, and I won't wait for her any longer. She's always dragging me along on these outings, then expecting me to wait for her. Perhaps you could give me a lift to the same place you're going?" She gifted him with a sultry smile and the young man's glasses almost dropped off his nose. She moved closer and touched a hand to his arm. It was warm and well-muscled. "In fact, why don't we go somewhere dark and quiet." She raised a brow. "Just you and I?" Her bag dropped to the ground and her hand wound up around his neck, while her other hand slid up under his loose cotton shirt.

If she couldn't have Alara's blood tonight, this one would suffice.

****

A loud bang on her door had Alara springing upright in bed.

"Alara!"

She recognized Sam's voice and almost tripped over the edge of her sheet in her haste to get to the door.

"What is it?" She tore the door open and pushed sleep-tousled hair from her eyes. "What are you doing here, and what the hell time is it? Has the sun even risen yet?"

Sam eyed the sheet wrapped around her body. "Get dressed. You're needed downstairs."

She frowned. "Downstairs. I don't understand." Nothing was registering. Her brain was still asleep. Sam should know her mind didn't click into gear until she'd swallowed her morning dose of caffeine. She headed for her room and scooped her crumpled jeans and tee from the floor, tossing them onto the bed. She began to dress. "What is this all about?" Alara could hear Sam pottering around in the kitchen. Perhaps he did know her well enough after all.

She finished pulling on her shirt, picked up her gun

and holster, and marched into the kitchen. Sam scooped two teaspoons of instant coffee into two mugs and filled them with steaming hot water. He added three sugars to hers and pushed it into her hand. She took an appreciative sniff and a sip, set the coffee on the bench, and sat to pull on her sneakers.

"There's been a murder," Sam finally answered. "I think it's the guy who lives next door to you."

Alara frowned and picked up her mug, then put it back down without drinking. "What kind of murder?" She had a terrible feeling in the pit of her stomach. She knew the answer before it came.

"Two puncture wounds in his neck. His blood drained." Sam's brow rose. "Sound familiar?"

She swallowed the boulder in her throat. "Vampire. Do you think the bites are real? What about the press?"

"We've been able to keep them at bay so far, but it's only a matter of time before something's leaked. And yes, the bite is the same as the other two." Sam ran a hand back through his thick wavy hair. "What is going on here, Alara? First the girl who looks like you, now your neighbor?"

Alara took several large swallows of coffee and tipped the rest down the sink. "I don't know, but I will promise you this. If I find the bastard, who did it, I'll stake him to the ground in the sun and watch the fucker burn." She slammed her cup onto the bench and headed for the door. "Coming?"

She descended the stairs to the ground floor to find it crawling with cops. She located the head of forensics, with Sam close behind her. "Anything, Fudge?"

The elderly white-haired gentleman shook his head. "Only a few drops of blood on the victim's shirt.

We're sending the shirt back to the lab for testing. We'll see if we can get some DNA.

"Estimated time of death?"

"From the state of the body, between ten and eleven p.m."

Alara nodded. Just after Epatha had left her apartment. A twinge of suspicion nagged at her brain, but she pushed it aside, classifying it as ridiculous. "Do me a favor will you, Fudge?"

The old man smiled. "Of course, my dear. You know you're my favorite lady detective."

Alara smiled back. "Give me a call as soon as you know anything."

Fudge nodded. He was about to turn away but swung back. "Oh, about that key you found in that cabin. We had it traced to a safe deposit box at the New York City Bank."

Alara's heart leapt and for a moment she remained speechless. This was the break she had been searching for. She was sure the key belonged to *him*. She released the breath she was holding. "Thanks, Fudge. I owe you one."

"A bottle of scotch will be fine," he called back over his shoulder as he walked away.

"Will do." She spun to face Sam. "Did you hear that? The key belongs to a safe deposit box. It could tell us who he is."

"And it might not. Don't get your hopes up. I'll dial reception and get them to book us a flight this afternoon. However, the key could still belong to Lance MacManus's great grandfather you know."

She shook her head. "It's his. My gut tells me it is."

"And your gut is never wrong, right?" Sam shook his head and took her arm. "Come on, detective sergeant, I'll buy you that cup of coffee you never finished, and perhaps, just perhaps, we might be able to discuss this rationally."

****

Vincent stepped from the bathroom, drying the back of his hair and neck as Charlie let himself into the hotel room and switched on the light. The boy jumped at the sight of him.

"Don't you ever turn on lights?"

"What for? I can see just as well in the dark."

"Yeah. Well, I can't." Charlie moved to the bed, flopped the suitcase he carried up onto the bedspread and flicked the locks. The case was filled to capacity with money. "There's currency in here of every denomination dating back to the seventeen hundreds." He strode over to the fridge, pulled out a coke, downed a few mouthfuls and gave a loud belch. "I nearly couldn't fit all the money in the case. The backpack I had was too small. I bought the suitcase and went back. Then, the chick at the bank looked at me funny when she realized I was taking all of it. She insisted on being in the room with me. I think she thought I was stealing it, but couldn't prove anything, seeing I had a key. Then, when I was leaving, I saw your girlfriend. You didn't tell me she was a cop."

He tossed his towel onto a chair, picked up his black jeans from the bed and pulled them up over his hips. "You saw Alara at the bank?" He zipped up his pants and buckled his belt.

Charlie nodded. "Yeah, she was with a guy with sandy hair and two uniformed police officers. I saw her showing the manager her badge. Looks like she had a key to something, but I didn't stick around in case she recognized me from the night you were with her at the club."

He swore softly. "She must have found the key in the cabin." *Christ.* He ran a hand through his hair. He had to think. What exactly was in the box—a lot of memories. He shook his head—and plenty with his name on it. "Fuck," he swore out loud.

"Where'd you get all this?" Charlie ignored his profanity and ran his fingers through the money. Picking up a gold coin, he dropped it back into the case and turned several of the bills over to read the dates. "Guess that's a stupid question. I suppose you had plenty of time to save. Some of this stuff must be worth a fortune." He looked up as if studying Vincent for a reaction. "I know a guy who might be interested in buying some of these early bills and antique coins. If you are interested in selling, that is?"

He strolled over to the wardrobe, drew a black sweater from a hanger, and pulled it over his head. "Sure. It is not much use to me the way it is, and I will need a house. I cannot stay here indefinitely."

Charlie stuffed a couple of packets of old pound notes and a handful of gold coins into his jacket pockets and headed for the door. "I'll see if I can catch Rick at his shop. It might still be open. I'll be back later."

"And I am low on blood," Vincent called. "Can you procure some of that before you return?"

Charlie stopped at the door but didn't turn. "Sorry, man." He wouldn't look at Vincent. "I can't get anymore. The thefts have been noticed and they have really tightened security. I can't risk getting caught, or it could mean Kate's job. But I'll work something out. Promise."

He slipped into the hall before Vincent could respond and he was left contemplating the closed door. He flopped down in the chair by the window and stared into the night.

This was all he needed. Alara in his safe deposit box, and now he had to fetch his own dinner.

****

Alara arrived back at the office after catching an afternoon flight from New York. Sam had argued that she could search through the contents of the box in the morning. *Was he crazy?* She hadn't waited this long, nursed the box all the way from New York, to have it locked in evidence overnight.

She had lifted the hinged lid only once and that had been after removing it from the safe deposit box in the bank to check the contents. There had been a picture of a blonde woman in a wedding dress on top of a pile of papers. She'd dropped the lid again, quickly, but not before noting the uncanny resemblance to herself in the old photograph. That alone had niggled at her all the way back to Seattle.

She arranged the green, tin box on her desk almost reverently and pulled back the lid, just as Sam entered the office with two cups of take-out coffee he'd purchased from the diner across the road.

"I still don't know why we're doing this tonight." He set the coffee on the desk beside hers. "Aren't you tired? I am."

"Of course, I'm tired, but did you really think I'd wait?"

He lifted a brow and offered her a cup, but she

shook her head and gave him a glare.

"Aren't you just a little bit curious?" she coaxed, looking down again at the picture of the woman in the wedding dress.

Sam shrugged and reached for the photo, studied it for a moment, then frowned and held it up against her face. "I don't know if it's me, but this woman could be you. Different hair style, different era, but…"

"Yeah, I know. Uncanny, isn't it?" She took the picture from his hand and placed it on the desk. "I wonder if the name of our mystery woman is in here somewhere?" She lifted a few aged papers from the box. One was a deed to an antique shop in Sacramento made out in the name of Annabelle D'Armano. Annabelle. The same name as on the locket from the cabin. Coincidence? She didn't think so.

The next paper was a wedding certificate, yellowing and brittle, the writing spidery and almost faded. She could just make out two signatures. The first, which must have been the man's, was smudged beyond recognition. The second read, Annabelle Gale. Alara's heart slapped against her ribs, and Sam, realizing her grip on the paper was almost lethal, pried it from her fingers and held it up to the desk lamp to read.

"Annabelle Gale." He looked around and searched Alara's face. "Do you know her?"

"No." She lifted her chin meeting his dark-gray gaze. "But it is my last name."

"She might be a relation. Maybe, a great aunt?" He tried to help Alara back into her seat as her legs almost gave way, but she shrugged him off. Then she took the chair anyway. "I'm fine. It's just the shock of seeing her name." She lifted several more photos from the box, but all were of the woman, none of Annabelle's husband.

Sam leaned over and picked up another photo and shrugged. "It's odd that there's no pictures of this guy?"

"Not if he's a vampire."

"How could that be? I thought from everything I've heard and read of their kind vampires are cold-blooded killers. Why didn't he kill Annabelle?"

Alara shrugged. "Who's to say he didn't?" She slid a newspaper clipping from the top of the pile and read the headline. *Vampire style slaying. Woman murdered. Husband accused and missing!* She handed the article to Sam.

"If he did it, why keep the clipping, and why the box and pictures? It looks more like something someone would do out of love and respect, not the work of a murderer." Sam handed back the article.

Her lips thinned, and her tone held an edge, as she dropped it back onto her desk. "Don't go soft on me now, Sam. Make no mistake. This creature is a murderer. He killed Ice. I saw him flee the scene, and I will never forget that day, or the bloody wound in my lover's neck."

Sam touched Alara's shoulder. "I know," he soothed. "But you have to be rational about this. There's nothing in here that really proves this D'Armano guy is a vampire. We'll do a search on the woman and see what we can find on her murder, and her family. Perhaps she has relations."

Alara lifted the last few mementos from the box. Several more photos of Annabelle in an evening dress. "Look at these, Sam. The clothes are straight out of the forties."

"Yeah, I remember a hand-colored photo of my grandmother dressed in a pale blue gown like that."

Lastly, she took out a pressed blue flower, then a man's crimson bow tie.

She stared down at the faded bow tie in her hand, finding it hard to associate it with a blood sucking, cold-hearted vampire, then she dropped it back into the box. She was about to stack the rest of the papers in on top when she noticed a ring in the bottom corner. Sam saw it too, and snatched it up before her.

"It has a crest."

He held the ring beneath the light for her to see. Alara could make out the raised head of a wolf on a rose background.

"We'll get this traced and dated." He reached for a brown paper bag on his desk. "It might confirm the name of our vampire."

"So, now you admit he is a vampire." Alara lifted a brow in satisfaction and closed the lid on the green box.

Sam swallowed his lukewarm coffee and stood. "Let's just say, I'm not ruling it out."

Chapter Seven

Alara drew her Pontiac Firebird to a halt across the road from her building at ten p.m. Since the murder, it gave her the heebie-jeebies to come home late. However, she had little choice, and now it seemed as if the whole night conspired against her. Over an hour ago it had begun to spit, and now that had changed to a steady chilling drizzle. The night was pitch black, and by the light of a lone streetlamp on the corner, only one other parked car was visible.

She slid from her vehicle, locked the door, and proceeded to cross the road. Halfway to the footpath she sensed him. A chill prickled her neck, then transformed to a feeling of warm comfort and a sense of arousal so strong she could barely suppress it. She stopped mid-stride and searched the night. Alara could swear she saw a large wolf standing in the darkness alongside her building. Then Vincent stepped from the shadows to be revealed in the light streaming through the glass door. He was by far the most handsome man she had ever known.

It was three days since she'd seen him.

Three days too long.

She sought to still her quaking body and force one foot in front of the other.

His long black coat brushed the rain-drenched pavement and was open to expose dark jeans and sweater, and the very maleness of him consumed her. How could she ever have sent him away? She loved this man. She knew it now as strongly as she knew roses needed the rain to survive. She needed his touch. She didn't really know him, knew nothing about him except she wanted him in her bed and his body wrapped around her, in her. Comforting, telling her all was right with the world.

She gained the footpath and stopped before him. He was taller than she remembered, seeming to tower over her. His long black fringe fell forward into his soulful dark eyes, and she reached up with both hands to brush his hair back from his face. "Why didn't you wait inside? You're drenched."

"You said I was not welcome."

She lowered her hands to her sides, her excitement turning to a hurtful lump in her chest. "Then why did you come here?"

"Because…I could not stay away." His arms closed around her, and he dragged her up close. His kiss when it came was raw, sensual, and stripped Alara's soul bare, exposing her vulnerability. And the heavens opened up with a deluge of icy rain.

However, she felt no cold as a molten river of pure pleasure erupted within her core at the first taste of Vincent's rain wet mouth.

His lips on her eyelids, ears, and exposed throat did dangerous things to her lower belly, and all she wanted was to crawl into him and lose herself forever. She pushed her hands inside his coat and up across his hard, muscled, chest. His skin was cold, grave cold and the sensation on her fingers snapped her from her world of pleasure back into reality. How long had he waited here in the rain?

"We better get you inside," she said, dragging her mouth reluctantly from his, and leaning her cheek against his shoulder. "You will catch your death. You're freezing." She rubbed at his back, trying to infuse some heat into his body.

His lips touched her ear. "I do not feel cold." There was a smile in his voice.

"Well, I do." She drew from his arms and took his hand, leading him up the stairs into the foyer, but as they reached the landing, he pulled her to him and scooped her into his arms.

She gave a small squeal. "What are you doing?"

"Carrying you," he said, moving toward the stairs with an easy gait.

"I'm too heavy."

By way of answer, he dropped a small kiss on her nose and took the first flight at a run. He hit the landing without breaking a sweat, set her on her feet and backed her against the wall, taking her mouth in a heat-filled kiss. Then before she could speak, he lifted her again and raced up the next flight without resting. On the second floor, his lips slid across her throat, her eyelids, and his mouth claimed hers in a hard kiss that told her so many things, but most of all, that he was hers.

Before she could speak, before she could draw breath, they were again on their way. They hit the third floor and Vincent strode down the hallway to her apartment. He lowered her and backed her against the wall, their breath joining as one, his firm body molded intimately to hers, his hands beneath her shirt, cupping her breasts, his tongue hot in her ear.

"I have to catch my breath," she gasped. "I have to

find the key. Please, stop. I can't think."

He stepped back, and she searched in her bag, her hand closing over the key.

"You are not going to stop me coming in?" His gaze met hers, and the raw sensuality in his eyes made Alara's hand tremble. In fact, her whole body trembled.

"Of course, you can come in."

"Then relinquish me the key or we will be standing here all night instead of doing what we really want to do." His voice like deep rich chocolate had her insides melting all over again. He took the key from her hand and fitted it to the lock. The door swung open, and he stepped aside for her to move into the room and followed.

****

She crossed the room graceful as a cat, lithe, surefooted. She flicked on the lamp, then pulled back the drapes. The night was black, the harbor ablaze with lights, and rain slashed at the window. At least something good was about to happen on one rainy night in his life.

"I don't think we need this, do you?" Vincent killed the lamp, then moved faster than intended, reaching her in warp speed. He just wanted her, just wanted to touch her, wanted to bury himself within her and live there always. He had satisfied his other hunger earlier; now he would satisfy this one. He slipped out of his coat and tossed it to the couch. Before he could reach for her, she was drawing his sweater over his head and running her hands up over his chest. "You're still cold."

"Poor circulation." He clutched the bottom of her wet T-shirt and pulled it from her body. "However, we need to get you into a shower." He saw her shiver and scooped her, weightless, into his arms. She gave a small squeal, and he carried her into the bathroom, lowered her, and reached for the taps.

"Only if you join me," she offered, spanning his waist to unbuckle his jeans and lower his zipper.

He spun, reclaiming her lips, and crushed her to him as the room filled with hot, moist steam. He wanted her badly, needed her. The clasp of her bra melted beneath his fingers, and he filled his hands with her firm, warm breasts. Taking one into his mouth he tasted her, drawing on her large, pink nipple. Then he dropped to his knees and trailed soft wet kisses down her stomach until he came to the fastening of her pants. That too was no hindrance, and he pushed her jeans down over her silky-smooth thighs and pressed his face against the sheath of her black G-string. Her scent drove him to a frenzy. He tore the soft piece of cloth asunder and dropped it to the white fur rug. With both hands firmly clutching her derrière, he drew her toward his mouth.

His tongue flicked over her bud and her taste was intoxicating. He heard her groan, and she stiffened as if in protest, but the sound only urged him on.

She clung to his shoulders and shifted her stance.

His tongue slipped up inside her, and again he ran his tongue across her cleft, this time tantalizingly slow. His whole mouth closed over her, feasting, driving her on harder, higher, and faster. He felt her orgasm when it came and held her closer enjoying her pleasure, but he wanted more. Coming to his feet he stripped off his jeans and in one fluid movement, lifted Alara so her legs spanned his waist and stepped into the steaming shower.

He lowered her to sheath his body. Flesh against flesh, man against woman. She was hot, wet, and fit him just right, and if his first shower in the hotel room the night Charlie had taken him there had been close to heaven, he knew now, this was the real thing.

****

Alara had died and gone to heaven. This man was her salvation. All those years alone in purgatory after Ice then Ruth's death, washed away by the touch of his hands.

She took his lips with savage hunger. Water, heat, red wine, and her, that was his taste. When he'd taken her into his mouth outside the shower, she hadn't known what to do. It was the first time a man had done that to her; not even with Ice had she experienced such a thing. The intensity of her feelings had overwhelmed her, frightening her, delighting her all in one. It had felt so right. He had brought her to fulfillment so quickly, the same as he was doing right now. His powerful body filling her so completely, all velvet and hardness. She couldn't breathe. Her head rested on his shoulder as he moved and braced himself against the shower wall, water streaming down and around them, and his hard body slamming into hers.

Then she felt it again, that quivering sensation building, lifting her higher, filling her.

He held her tight, as her body gave a final spasm. She cried out as she felt his release, and he crushed her to his chest to ride out the storm.

However, he was not finished yet.

He lowered her to the floor, took a handful of shower gel, and proceeded to wash every part of her body. His hands lingered diligently over the roundness of her breasts and the soft swell of her belly. Then his long slender fingers trailed down between her thighs as his mouth took hers in a drugging kiss, and he made her explode all over again.

Finally, he turned off the water, stepped from the shower, and wrapped her in a large fluffy towel.

"Warm now?" he asked, looking down at her, his dark wet hair dripping into his Heathcliff eyes.

What could she do, but smile?

****

Alara opened her eyes just before dawn to find him by her bed. "You're leaving?" Disappointment hit her like a boulder in the stomach. She didn't know why she thought he would stay. She just had. "I have the day off. I thought we could go to the beach for a picnic. The weather hasn't been that great but..."

"Sorry." He shook his head.

She pushed into a sitting position, the sheet held close to her breasts. Breasts he had worshipped for half the night. She dispelled the thought from her mind, and bit down on her lower lip. "Why?" She frowned, the word sounding harsher than intended. "Did I do something wrong?"

He sank onto the side of the bed and took her hand in his, studying each finger in turn. Then he dropped a small kiss into her palm. "It is not that I do not want to stay, but I must work."

"What job requires you to start so early?" Her hand crept up inside his sweater. His abs were so hard, not an ounce of fat.

"I'm contracting a stockbroker for a Tokyo firm. I have to be at my office when the market opens."

"Oh." She pushed his long fringe back from his eyes, luxuriating in the feel of his silky dark hair running through her fingers. "Will I see you tonight?"

"About eight." His demanding lips caressed hers and seared a path down her neck and across to her shoulder. He moved over her, his body pinning her to the bed, hard, powerful, fitting her contours perfectly. Her breasts chafed achingly against the cloth of his soft woolen sweater. "Tonight." His whisper touched her lips, then he was off the bed and through the door before she could say another word.

She sighed and lay back on her pillows, luxuriating in all the pleasurable pains in her body that told of his touch, and relived again the magical night of ecstasy they'd shared. However, the only thing that marred her thoughts was the fact that they had not used protection. As a modern-day detective, she would have expected better of herself, yet both times she had been caught up in the passion of the moment. No excuse, she knew, but it was the only one she could give. She would grab a morning after pill at the pharmacy. But she smiled inwardly. Would it be so bad anyway, to have a little, black-haired Vincent running around her apartment?

Then her thoughts came crashing back to reality with the harsh call tone of her cell phone.

She reached for the receiver. "Hello."

"Alara. Epatha. Sorry for calling so early. How about catching up for that drink tonight?"

****

Sam glanced up as Alara rushed into the office for the third consecutive morning and stuffed her handbag into the pigeonhole in her desk. "What?" She glared as she caught him staring and collapsed into her chair.

"You look like death warmed over." He passed her the box of doughnuts and the rest of his coffee. "For someone who hardly drinks, you sure look like you're hung over."

Blood heated her cheeks, and she shook her head at the doughnuts but downed the last two mouthfuls of his coffee. It tasted like dishwater. "Vincent came over last night. I guess I got to sleep a bit late." She looked down at the paperwork on her desk, hoping her face was not as crimson as it felt.

"So, you're still seeing him."

She glanced up, holding his gaze. "Is there a problem with that?"

"I thought you said it was over."

"And if it isn't?"

Sam raised his hands and backed up. "Nothing. But...have you ever thought how strange it is that Vincent's name starts with a V, the same as the guy we are looking for? There's not many names beginning with V. Only Victor and Vincent that I can think of. And do you even know his last name? You've never mentioned it. And he did look a bit pale the night I met him. Almost sickly."

"His hair and eyes are dark," she bit back. "It makes his skin look pale. He's not sick—" she paused, "—or I don't think he is. He doesn't act sick." She blushed again and looked away.

Sam's left eyebrow raised fractionally. "Have you seen him in the daylight?"

She lifted her chin, and her lips thinned. "He works early, and I work late, as you do."

"Where does he work?"

"He's a stockbroker," she responded with

confidence. "He told me the other morning." Still, there was so much she didn't know about him. "Look, I've had enough of this. You're being ridiculous. You're being paranoid and putting doubts in my head." She came to her feet and shuffled a few papers, not really looking at them. "Of course, Vincent isn't a vampire." She chuckled. "He even has a sister. Epatha. I'm meeting with her tonight for drinks. She's quite a stunner, around thirty." It was Alara's turn to raise a brow as she settled back into her chair. "Not married from what I know. How about it? Why don't you tag along, and we can both quiz her on Vincent's name, rank, and serial number." She gave him a saccharine smile.

He rested back in his chair and studied her with an expressionless face as if mulling the possibility over in his mind. "I might just do that." He stood and came over to stand beside her. "Where are we meeting?"

Caught unaware, Alara paused to think. "The diner in the Plaza, on Fifth, at seven p.m. The Giggi Café, I think it's called."

Sam jotted down the name and time on a notepad he pulled from his shirt pocket. "Done. Now can we get down to business? I got some information back on the ring we discovered in the box. Fudge sent it to a professor friend of his, who deals in antique jewelry. He was able to trace it back to an ancient and distinguished Venetian family by the name of D'Armano. Their line died out in the 1790s with the mysterious death of the father and daughter and the disappearance of the son, Vincent."

Warning bells rang in Alara's head. Hadn't Vincent said he was born in Venice as the sun set over the water? A shiver sprinkled her nape. Evidence was certainly mounting up, but she pushed it aside. *Now who is being ridiculous? It can't be my Vincent.* "It must be a coincidence," she answered. "What about the DNA? Did forensics find anything on the shirt they took from my neighbor? Or the box from the bank?"

Sam laughed shortly. "Yeah, but it doesn't add up."

Alara frowned. "What are you talking about? What doesn't match?"

"Fudge managed to take saliva samples from the victim in the cabin, the one in the park, and in your foyer. The last two match, but not the one from the MacManus murder."

"So, what are you saying? That there's not one vampire, but two?"

"If you had asked me that same question four weeks ago, I would have called you insane, but now…" He shrugged, leaving the sentence hanging. "And there is more. I think you better take a look at the samples we took from the bodies. They are nowhere near normal. I've never seen anything like them. Fudge says both perpetrators must be totally anemic."

"If they are vampires of course they're anemic, hence the need for blood."

"Which takes us back to your boyfriend. Do you ever see him eat? Has he ever bitten your neck?"

"Of course, he hasn't bitten my neck," she snapped, giving him a hard stare. "You're ridiculous. He's not a vampire. He couldn't be. From what I know of vampires, they are cold-blooded killers. He has never harmed a hair on my head." However, deep down Alara realized she had never seen Vincent eat, other than to drink a glass of red wine. He always said he'd eaten earlier when she mentioned food. He wouldn't even take coffee. A chill swept down her back, and as much as she wanted to quash her traitorous thoughts, she couldn't. Was the man she loved, the man she could barely stand to be apart from, one and the same as the enemy she had hunted half her life? She shook her head. How ironic, and if so, what danger did he now pose for her?

****

Epatha stubbed out her third cigarette and glanced around the room. Smoking. An unhealthy vice, she knew. One she suspected she would already be dead from had she not been virtually immortal.

Seated at a table in the center of the diner, surrounded by a sea of living breathing humanity, the stink of them, the sound of the blood pounding through their veins was almost unbearable. Why had she agreed to this? Why couldn't the woman have accorded her the decency to meet at the bar she'd suggested? It was quiet, tolerable…had a small narrow alley out back.

It was lucky she had feasted on a piece of human vermin down at the docks or she would now be grabbing the pristine little waiter. He had stuck the menu under her nose three times already, asking if she would like to order. Yes, she would like to order, she mused. Waiter, naked on a white platter.

She lit up her fourth cigarette and took a deep drag. Glancing up she watched Alara step through the door followed by a tall sandy-haired man in jeans, blue shirt, and dark-gray, leather jacket. She exhaled her smoke in a rush. Now what? Wouldn't this girl ever be available so she could kill her and get it over with?

Alara spied Epatha as she raised her hand in

greeting and led the man toward her with a smile on her face. She rose to take her hands and drop a small kiss on both cheeks, when all she wanted to do was sink her teeth into the girl's soft white throat.

"Epatha, I would like you to meet my partner, Sam Grayson. He was feeling lonely, so I brought him along."

"You make me sound desperate." Sam grinned.

"Sam." Epatha nodded her head in Sam's direction and gifted him a seductive smile.

"Those things will kill you," he said, indicating her cigarette.

"So, I have heard." She smiled again, a little more brittle and settled back into her chair to stub out her offending smoke.

"Shall we order?" Sam asked, picking up the menu. "I'm famished. We just finished work. And one can only live on coffee and doughnuts for so long." He looked across at Epatha.

She grimaced accordingly. "Anything interesting happening in Seattle I should know about?" She ran her finger around the edge of her wine glass, making light conversation. She supposed since she was trapped here, she may as well find out what they knew about her latest two victims.

She glanced up as Sam lowered the menu to look straight at her. "As a matter of fact, there is. We think we have a vampire on the loose."

Epatha coughed almost spitting the mouthful of wine she had just taken all over the tablecloth. "You must be joking. I thought vampires were creatures of myth, stories to frighten people around campfires, or children on stormy nights?" She lowered her glass and widened her eyes, feigning innocence. "How frightening, I must remember to buy some garlic and bolt my windows tonight." She lifted her wine to the light to watch it turn to blood red. "Any suspects?"

"A couple."

She saw Alara throw Sam a terse look.

"But nothing definite," he elaborated, "and that's enough about work." He motioned to the waiter. "I'm sure we have more pleasant matters to discuss."

Epatha released a small sigh. The look Sam had given her almost had her believing he suspected *her*. She slid a veiled glance at both detectives. If she needed to take two out tonight, she was sure she could do it. It would not be the first time, but she would prefer not to expend that much energy. She took another sip of wine. Deep, rich, and slightly acidic, it reminded her of the blood she had drunk earlier. The blood she would drink later.

The waiter that had been bothering her arrived back at the table, order book in hand, and she gave him an earthy smile.

"What would you ladies like? My treat." Sam encompassed both women in his gaze. "I backed a winner today and I feel like celebrating."

"I thought you gave up the horses?" Alara's tone was curt, and the light went from Sam's eyes.

"Not now, Alara."

"Nothing for me." Epatha smiled. It was becoming continually hard trying to keep up this subterfuge, when all she wanted to do was leap across the table and have them for dinner. "I had a large lunch."

"But you must. Alara and I won't feel right eating in front of you. Coffee, then, I insist."

"Fine, an espresso." She had never drunk coffee in her long life. She thought it a vile smelling substance, but anything to get the man off her back. No matter his jovial mood, for some uncanny reason she had the feeling he was testing her.

"And Alara? Your usual?"

The blonde girl nodded.

"Good." Sam snapped the menu closed. "A T-bone, rare, with fries and an egg, a chicken salad, two glasses of Chardonnay, and an espresso for the beautiful lady across the table." He thanked the waiter and handed back the menu.

Alara turned to Epatha. "I was wondering if you've seen Vincent. I'm still trying to catch up with him. I haven't seen him since the night of the party."

Epatha frowned wondering why the girl was lying. She had distinctly seen Vincent leaving Alara's apartment three days in a row this week. "No, I haven't." Her reply was short.

"Maybe we could put a trace on him." Sam smiled. "All we need is a last name. I don't believe you mentioned your last name when we were introduced. Alara told me you and Vincent were brother and sister?"

Epatha sucked in her breath. What were these two up to? She took a mouthful of wine to bide her time. Did Alara and Sam suspect her? Surely not. She hardly knew the girl, and this was the first time she had met Sam.

She slid a glance from one to the other. They were studying her expectantly, waiting for an answer. Well, she would give them one, but they were not getting *her* last name, even if she had one. "D'Armano," she replied, throwing Vincent to the wolves.

"D'Armano?" Sam pounced. "I do believe that's Venetian. Yet your accent isn't Italian."

"No, it is Egyptian. I was born in Egypt before our parents moved to Venice."

"Vincent's accent is English. How do you explain that?" Alara leaned back as her meal was placed in front of her.

Epatha waited for her coffee to be set down and looked across appreciatively at the rich bloody juice pooling around Sam's steak. He cut into the meat, and she unconsciously licked her lips. "My mother was English. We migrated to London after Vincent's birth."

"I see." Alara stared down at her food without touching it, and a silence settled over the table.

"Look." Sam shoveled a forkful of steak and fries into his mouth. "Isn't that Vincent by the door? I wonder how he knew we were here?" He glanced at Alara.

****

Alara's heart skipped several beats. Of all the bad timing. She rose and wound her way through the tables and patrons toward him. As if he knew she were there, he spun and pinned her with his dark Heathcliff gaze. Then he looked to Sam and Epatha at the table and his expression darkened.

What did one say to her lover when she had just discovered he was a vampire and could have killed the most precious person in her life?

He tried to kiss her as she reached him, but she turned her head, and his lips grazed her cheek.

"What has she been saying?" he asked. His jaw set hard. "I told you not to meet with her. She is dangerous."

Alara stared into his eyes. They were like twin pools of darkness. As dark as the soul he didn't have. "How is she dangerous, Vincent? I don't believe you explained last time?"

"She is a vicious liar. You cannot believe a word she says." He looked over her shoulder. "Can we just get out of here?"

Alara sensed he was uncomfortable, but she was not about to go anywhere with him, alone, just yet. "I'm eating. I can't just leave. So, you either join me, or—"

He strode past her toward the table without answering. His face like carved marble. How had she not noticed his pallor before? She could sense he wasn't happy, but neither was she. There were too many unanswered questions between them.

"Sam. Epatha." He nodded to both occupants, removed his coat, and settled into the chair the waiter had placed at the table on seeing his intention to join them.

Nobody spoke, but Alara did notice Epatha sugaring her coffee, and Vincent watching with narrow eyes.

"Would you like coffee?" Sam looked at him.

"I do not drink coffee." Vincent answered, his tone expressionless.

"Tea, then?"

"I do not drink tea, either."

"Then what do you drink, *or* eat?" Sam asked laying aside his knife and fork, looking directly into his eyes.

Epatha gave a small cough. "Sam and Alara have been telling me about a most fascinating case they are working on." Epatha peered at Vincent over the edge of her cup as she lifted her coffee to her lips. "It has to do with vampires." She raised a finely arched brow.

Alara could have cut the air with a knife.

"Is that so?" Vincent's gaze met hers, and for a fleeting moment the anguish in his eyes as he looked at her almost made her cry out. Then he picked up the menu the waiter had left and signaled that he was ready to order.

The hovering waiter was there in a flash.

"A steak, rare, with a Caesar salad, and a glass of Sauvignon, thank you." The menu snapped shut. He handed it back and looked straight at Sam, as if to say, satisfied.

Sam just shoveled another forkful of steak and egg into his mouth as if nothing had happened. Couldn't he see she was dying here, that her world was falling apart? She pushed her plate aside and took a large swallow of her Chardonnay, then blinked as the stone in Epatha's pendant flashed into her eyes. It had been tucked down the woman's open-necked shirt, but a movement had brought it into view.

"What a lovely ruby," she said without thinking. "How does it work? It seems to light up. How unusual. I've seen you wear it before, but I've never seen it glow like that."

Epatha looked at Vincent before answering. "Oh, this old thing." She drew out the jewel from inside her shirt and held it toward Alara. "It is an antique. Passed down to me from a very old friend of our family. You remember Uncle Imohn, don't you, Vincent? He told me the stone was unearthed in a tomb of an Egyptian Pharaoh. *King Tuthmosis III*, I believe." The dark-haired woman laughed shortly. "It is reputed to be magic, but I have never seen it do anything special except light up. I am always being called upon to explain the phenomenon. Maybe it might be easier to leave the jewel at home next time." She dropped it back down her shirt.

"It would be a shame," said Alara, taking a sip of wine. "It's a beautiful piece."

Epatha gave Alara what looked like a forced smile, finished her coffee, and picked up the small chocolate on the side of her saucer to nibble on. Vincent's meal arrived, and he cut into his rare steak and brought the fork to his mouth, eyeing Sam coldly.

Perhaps they had been wrong. She kicked Sam under the table, but he just looked at her as if to say, wait and see.

However, Vincent finished his steak, salad, and wine without incident. As the waiter took his plate, he slid a fifty-dollar note from his pocket and placed it on the table. "Coming?" He looked pointedly at Alara, rose, and donned his coat.

"I haven't got my car. Sam gave me a lift."

"We can take a cab."

"Don't bother, I can drop you home." Sam finished his wine and stood. "Where do you live?"

"I thought I would come back to your place for a while." Vincent hadn't lifted his gaze from Alara.

"I—" Sam started.

"It's all right, Sam. That'll be fine." She turned to Epatha who had yet to rise. The dark-haired woman had a sullen look on her face, but when she realized Alara was looking, forced a smile.

"I'll linger here a little longer and have another red.

Who knows." She spread her arms. "The night is young. I might get lucky."

Lucky at what? Alara wondered. If the woman was a vampire, she really didn't fancy leaving her to pounce on her next unsuspecting victim, but she had little choice. "We'll catch up, then."

"I will call."

Alara nodded.

"Are you sure you don't need a ride?" Sam dropped several notes onto the table to cover the rest of the check.

"Very." Epatha signaled to the waiter and ordered another sauvignon as they walked away.

They reached the door together, but Sam stopped. "Would you mind if I had a private word with Alara, Vincent?" He gave the dark-haired man a friendly pat on the shoulder. "It's about work. I'll only take a moment of her time, then she'll be all yours." He winked.

Vincent nodded, and Alara moved several paces ahead with Sam.

"What's this about?" She turned her back to Vincent.

"What do you think? You are going home with a damned vampire."

"We don't know that for certain." Alara's lips thinned. "He ate the steak and salad, didn't he?"

"That's no proof and you know it. The steak was rare, and what about his name?"

"I *don't* want to talk about this now, Sam. I'll make up my own mind." She took a step away, but Sam grabbed her arm and pulled her back.

"Here, take this." He moved so that Alara's body

shielded his movements and pulled his Glock 19 from the leather holster beneath his jacket. He pushed it into her open handbag. His gray eyes met her green ones. "The bullets are silver. From what I've read, they will kill their kind. And *don't* let him stay. I'm sitting guard outside your place. I'll follow when he leaves. We need to find his lair."

Alara's jaw hardened. "I'll do it, but I don't like it. I'm still not sure…"

He squeezed her hand. "I know, but I don't like you with him on your own until we *are* sure. Promise."

"Fine." She gave him a stiff nod and hurried back to Vincent. "Ready?" she asked brightly. Too brightly and allowed him to take her hand. However, she could not ignore the coldness of his flesh, and the world-weary look in his dark eyes.

Chapter Eight

The night was balmy and full of stars. Vincent slipped from the back of Sam's old Chevy and waited for Alara to alight from the front seat. He thanked the other man for the ride, took Alara's hand, and watched the detective drive away into the night. They crossed the road in silence and climbed the stairs.

Vincent thought Alara a little withdrawn but put it down to the awkward evening with Epatha. Also, she'd put in a tiring day. She stopped in front of her door, about to reach for the key in her handbag, but he wrapped his arms around her waist to draw her back against him. It had been so long since he'd kissed her. He felt like a man thirsting for life, and it had nothing to do with his blood lust, which he'd appeased earlier that evening.

Alara slipped from his embrace and turned.

"Something wrong?" He shoved his hands into his coat pockets with a sinking feeling in his gut. "If this is about Epatha? I'm—"

"No." She lowered her head so he could not read her eyes and continued to search her handbag. "It isn't Epatha. I'm just tired. It might be best if you don't stay tonight."

Vincent thought he caught a glimpse of something metallic in her bag as he watched. A gun—but of course Alara would have a gun. She was a detective.

"How did you know I was in that restaurant?" she asked, pinning him with her emerald-green gaze, key in hand.

"I didn't. I wandered in for a bite to eat," he lied. He knew she was at the restaurant. He'd found her apartment empty and searched for her. He could track her scent anywhere, and with the speed and senses of the wolf, he had little trouble locating her. But something about tonight wasn't right. The vibe she was giving off. The way she had acted in the restaurant, quiet, distracted, and the odd questions from Sam about his eating habits.

He took Alara by the shoulders and drew her slowly into his arms. She relaxed into his body, her soft contours molding against his harder ones. Her heart beat into his chest like a butterfly trying to escape. He trailed soft wet kisses over her hair, her nape, and down the side of her throat, and felt her stiffen.

She spun and shoved at his chest. "Get away from me!"

The look on her face said it all.

He pushed his fringe from his eyes and met her gaze in the dim light, really looked at her. She was beautiful, fragile, and it was there in her face, in her wide green eyes. It was like a living thing, palatable, reaching out to him, like the fear in the wild creatures of the forest he had hunted. Like the terror of his victims before he had feasted in the old days. She was afraid of him. She knew what he was. He did not know how, but she knew. He sensed it.

And he had lost her.

Pain like a sharp stake struck his heart. Perhaps that would be preferable.

He wondered what had tipped her off. *The box of mementos from the bank? The pictures of Annabelle? The same name on the locket?* He had suspected Alara had the key, and now looking back, had he mentioned Annabelle's name, or had Epatha? He shrugged. What did it matter? She had likely put two and two together and knew he killed the boy in the cabin. She hadn't been promoted to detective sergeant for nothing. She was smart, his Alara. He shoved his hands into his pockets and studied her as she watched him. She held her body alert, as if expecting an attack, yet she hadn't reached for the gun. Perhaps there was still...he held out his hand about to speak, but Alara took a quick step backward.

He gave a short laugh and met her eyes. For a moment he just looked at her drinking in her image. "Goodbye, Alara," he said softly, his words containing a note of the pain that tore at his heart. Her eyes widened in comprehension, and he drank in one last look of her delicate heart-shaped face. A face he would remember for all time.

"I would never have hurt you," he breathed. Then he turned and walked out of her life.

****

Alara watched him stride down the corridor and disappear around the corner, her heart going with him. Vampire or not, she had loved that man, even more so than Ice. Ice had been a young girl's dream. Vincent had been a woman's.

Finally, the shaking hand that held the key contacted the lock and she pushed open the door. Jesse came to greet her, but she ignored her cat for the first time ever, and without turning on the light stumbled her way to her bedroom. She dropped her bag to the floor, almost tripped over her slippers, pulled back the covers, and slid into her bed, fully clothed. The sheets smelled of him, the cologne he wore, deep, mysterious, notes of mountain air, the scent of his skin. She imagined his strong arms coming around her, holding her close as they had the night before. Whispering words of forever and always, kissing her hair, her eyes. His hands slipped lower to draw her against his body, and her throat closed over, and the tears came.

****

Vincent stepped out into the night and stopped under the glow of the light on the apartment building's porch. It was spitting rain, typical, as if the night had not been bad enough. He had lost his woman for being something he had no control over, he was going to get wet, and he felt sick. He had not eaten lettuce for over two hundred years, if he had ever eaten the horrid leafy stuff at all, and it was burning a hole in his stomach. He needed fresh blood to rid the taste from his mouth, and to top everything, Sam was watching him from across the road. To the mortal eye the detective would not be visible wrapped in the shadows. To one of his keen night sight and senses, Sam was easily discernible.

He pulled his coat collar up around his neck to ward off the cold drizzle, stepped out into the night, rounded the corner, took on his wolf form, and cut across the road into the park.

Let Sam track him now! The man deserved a good run for whatever lies he had told Alara at the restaurant, which Vincent was certain had served *him* no purpose.

****

Alara slept badly, tossing and turning all night,

kept awake by the rain and imagined shadows in the night. Once she'd awoken and thought she'd seen a dark figure standing by the window. It must have been a dream, for the windows and doors were locked.

Pulling the collar of her brown suede jacket closer about her body to ward of the elements, she ran down the steps of her building. It was seven a.m. and the rain persisted.

She crossed the road and drew her car keys from her pocket, fitted the key to the lock, and stifled a scream as a white-faced body fell sideways out of her car door to lean against her legs. She swallowed down the bile that rose to her throat, and with shaking hands stuffed the body back in her car and slammed the door. For several minutes she froze, then fumbled for her phone and punched in Sam's number.

"Hello?" Sam's familiar voice came from the other end.

"Sam. Sam, please…" She released a small sob. "Sam, I need you."

She pushed a hand through her hair, knowing as a detective, she should have been able to cope, but with everything that had happened with Vincent…

"Alara? What's wrong? What is it?"

"There's a body, Sam. In my car…there's a body. I know I should be able to deal with this…" She slid to a crouch beside her car, a hand across her stomach, tears filling her eyes. "But…I can't…not now."

"Listen. Go back to your apartment. Lock the door and stay put. I'll call the SPD and get them over there."

She nodded, then realized he couldn't see her. "I'll make you coffee." She tried to steady her voice, but a warm tear slid down her cheek. "One more thing." Her voice broke. "It was…It was the young waiter from the café."

A heavy silence filled the air before Sam spoke again. "Fuck! Is it a vampire bite?"

She nodded again. "Yes. Do you think he did this to punish me?"

"I don't know, Alara." Sam's tone gentled. "But we will find out. I lost him last night after he left. I had already rung an officer to collect Vincent's glass from the busboy before they washed it. I also instructed them to watch Epatha and once she left the diner grab her glass too.

"The glasses were taken to the precinct last night. If they match up with the DNA samples we already have, we'll know for certain which one is our killer."

****

Charlie flicked on the light, strode across the room, drew the curtains, and rounded to stare down at Vincent, still in bed. "What's this? No hot date with your lovely Alara tonight? I thought you and her were a real item. That you were going to live happily ever after into eternity together." He raised one tawny brow. "What happened?"

"Go away, Charlie. I am in no mood for your sarcasm." Vincent rolled over and used the switch beside his bed to flick off the light.

Charlie turned it on again. "I've got something for you." The boy lowered his backpack to the floor, carefully withdrew a bottle, and set it on the bedside table. "Pig's blood." He grinned. "The best in Seattle." He held up his hands as Vincent frowned. "I know it isn't the real deal, but that vampire dude on the television used to drink it. I guessed if it was all right for him—I figured those writers or producers must have done their homework. Right?"

Vincent grimaced and pushed his legs over the side of the bed. Already his canines were beginning to swell. He hadn't fed all day, and now awake his hunger was akin to acid eating at his gut. He lowered his gaze from Charlie's bright blue eyes to the pulse beating rapidly in the boy's throat, sensed the sweet blood coursing his veins, and imagined the taste on his tongue.

He reached for the bottle, pulled off the stopper, and took a long deep draught. Rich, heady, a lot like human blood.

"Can you get more?" he asked, wiping the back of his hand across his mouth.

"Sure, I have a friend who works at the abattoirs. I paid him two bucks for this one, no questions asked. I'm sure he can get more."

Vincent passed back the bottle. "Thanks, Charlie, I do not know what I would do without you." And it beat going out into the rain, he mused.

Charlie shrugged. "Don't go all gloomy on me now." He stuffed the bottle back into his backpack and flopped into the oversized armchair by the fireplace. Leaning forward he turned up the heat on the fake log fire. "Sorry about your girl. Want to talk about it?"

"No." He came to his feet, scooped a pair of dark blue jeans from the end of the bed, and pulled them up over his hips. "Did you find a house?"

"As a matter of fact, I did. Big, old, on the outskirts of town and in not too bad a shape." Charlie snatched up his backpack and pulled out a newspaper. He opened several pages and gave the paper to Vincent. "It says there—"he pointed"—it is one-hundred and twenty years old."

He stared down at a large rambling house reminding him of the house his father had once owned in Hampshire. The price tag read $980,000. "Have I this much money?" He glanced across at Charlie resting back in the brown floral armchair, his feet up on the footrest.

"That much, and more. You're rich, man. Filthy rich. There was a hell of a lot of money in that case. Old stuff, worth a fortune. Clive sold most of it at an auction, but he's still getting the coins appraised. I've also opened an account in your name at the Seattle West Bank. At first, they kicked up a ruckus because I had no ID for you. However, when they saw the money, they soon came around. I showed them my ID and informed them I was your business manager. Guess I must have checked out, because they told me you had to sign this paper to return to the bank and all would be legal." He pulled a passbook and a form from his bag and handed it to Vincent. "There's forty million dollars in that account." Charlie folded his hands in front of him and leaned forward in his chair, watching him. "I know you have lived a long time, but how does a vampire accumulate so much money?" He frowned. "Did you rob a dozen banks or something?"

"Or something." He allowed himself a smile, picked up a pen from the desk, signed the form, and handed it back to Charlie. Then folded the newspaper back in order. He had his own reasons for not wanting to think of those days. "I have done many things in my life, Charlie, of which I am not proud, and of which I would rather not speak. Buy the house."

"Can I live with you?" The boy grinned. "I can be

your Igor to your Dracula."

He gave a short laugh. "You do realize Dracula did not really exist. He was a work of fiction." He did not mention he had collaborated on the book. It would open up too many questions.

"Of course, I know that. But can I? Live with you that is." He grinned his infectious grin. "I know my sister would thank you from the bottom of her heart." To emphasize he held a hand to his chest.

"Why not. You are good company when you are not talking all the time." He glanced down at the paper ready to toss it onto the bed, when a small advertisement in the bottom right-hand corner leapt up at him in bold letters. *"Do You Want To Save Your Soul?"* "Hell!"

Charlie leaped to his feet and peered over his shoulder. "What is it? Someone else die?"

"No." Vincent raised the paper so he could read the small print. There was a man's name and a phone number.

Charlie flopped back into his armchair and Vincent picked up the phone and pushed it at him. "Call this number." He dropped the newspaper into the boy's lap. "Make an appointment. Tell him I want to see him, tonight. It is urgent."

Charlie glanced down at the name in the ad and laughed. "Dr. Red-Cloud. You've got to be kidding. With a name like that the man's got to be a fake."

"Call it, now," he ordered, his tone grave cold.

Charlie came from his chair, his expression serious. "You've got to be reasonable. What's he going to do? Put a Native American hex on you and give you back your soul? No one can do that." The boy shook his head. "I've heard of these people. They're quacks. Charlatans. Anything for a buck."

"I have to try. Please, just do it." Vincent sighed. He felt tired. More tired than he'd felt in over a hundred years. He missed Alara. And did not care what he would have to do to get her back.

Charlie released a harsh breath. "Okay, but don't say I didn't warn you."

****

Sam strode into the office as the police sketch artist rose to leave. Alara had sat with the artist since eight thirty a.m. The clock on the wall had just ticked over onto ten. She studied the sketch in her hand and turned the picture for Sam to see.

"The likeness is uncanny. You did a good job describing him." He grinned. "Yet again—"

"Don't say it, just don't, or I think I will shoot you."

The grin faded from Sam's face, and he stared down at the papers on his desk.

How could she not know what Vincent looked like? She carried his image in her heart. No matter what he was reputed to have been guilty of, or what he was, she would never forget him. "I'll get these to the printers today. I'll have them put in every club, hotel, and pub, and every newspaper in Seattle will carry his face on their front cover before tomorrow tonight. We missed today's copy. If we don't know where he lives yet, we soon will." She took a large gulp from the coffee on her desk. "Anything from forensics on the wine glasses? It's been two days since you took them up there. If those guys were any slower—"

"Whoa." Sam leaned over and waved a paper under

her nose. "Right here. I was about to read it." He laid it on his desk and Alara rose to read over his shoulder.

"It says the DNA taken from the last three victims belongs to the woman. The sample from the McManus kid belongs to Vincent." Sam glanced up, placing his hand over hers on his shoulder. "Sorry, but you knew it would go one way or the other. Just be thankful he isn't our serial killer."

A tight knot formed in her throat, and she swallowed. "No, but he still killed the McManus boy." She slipped her hand from beneath his and moved back to her desk to pick up the sketch. She stared down into Vincent's ageless eyes. Eyes full of secrets, eyes full of lies. She knew it was inevitable that truth would prevail. She had been ninety-nine percent certain he was a vampire. Her hunch had paid off, but the pain, the hurt and anger bit deep. He'd lied to her in so many ways. He had never told her he loved her, but his actions had made her believe. Is that what his kind did? Prey on lonely women? Make them fall in love with them, toy with them, then kill them?

She scooped up the drawing and strode from the room.

****

The night sky appeared clear, a cloak of black velvet with pinpoints of diamonds for accents. Vincent took this as an omen that all would go well with the meeting.

Charlie picked him up at eight in his sister's old blue convertible. The night Charlie had called, Red-Cloud the doctor had been out of town. Vincent had insisted he leave a message and the doctor called this morning to set up a meeting.

He felt skittish as a newborn foal. Was it really possible to win back one's soul, or was this man a charlatan as Charlie suspected?

The boy parked the car in a narrow street close to the docks. He slid from his seat and Charlie closed the roof and locked the doors.

A quaint shop sat across the road on the corner. The slightly askew sign above the door read *The Cozy Book Store*, and through the frosted glass door a dim light showed somewhere in a back room.

Vincent strode purposely across the road, then waited for Charlie to knock.

No answer came, so the boy knocked again.

The door opened several inches. "Yes?" said a voice with a slightly accented, Irish lilt.

"Doctor Red-Cloud?" inquired Charlie.

"Aye, that's who I be. Who might you be?"

"You're expecting us. I'm Charlie and this is Vincent." Charlie stood to the side, as a light came on in front of the store.

The doctor appeared to be close to sixty, had long gray hair, tied back in two plaits, one to each side of his gaunt cheeks. He stood tall, and wore a fringed white shirt, blue jeans, and knee-high moccasins. He took a step back as Vincent met his gaze and raised his hand as if to ward him off.

"Begone. Leave this place! I do not deal with your ilk." He tried to slam the door, but Charlie braced it with both hands to stop him.

"Vincent won't hurt you. He's not like others of his kind…please. He needs your help."

Red-Cloud opened the door a little farther and studied Vincent where he stood behind Charlie. "Is what the boy says true? I must admit it is unusual for one of the undead to be traveling in the company of a boy. What makes you so different?"

"I was cursed by a Cheyenne shaman."

The doctor gave a soft chortle. "Were you indeed? Then it seems you have come full circle." The old Native American ran his gaze the length of Vincent's body, then he shrugged his narrow shoulders. "Against my better judgment, I bid you enter. However, make no mistake, I am more than capable of a little cursing myself should the need arise." He stepped back into the shop and beckoned them to enter. He locked the door, then led them through a beaded curtain, down a passageway into a small cozy sitting room with two overstuffed dining chairs. A fire burned bright in a wide, open hearth, and a tepee about the height of a man's waist, fashioned from narrow sticks, took pride of place at the center of the room. Polished floorboards covered the floor, and a bearskin rug was set beneath the tepee.

Charlie moved to warm himself by the fire while Vincent stood just inside the doorway. He was not at all comfortable with the knowledge that the old man knew what he was.

"So, what do you wish of me?" The doctor's stance was alert, his arms crossed over his chest. His expression brooding.

Vincent took a step forward. "Is it as you say? Can you give a man back his soul?" He shoved his hands into his pockets to stop them from shaking. His future hung on this man's next words. Was it all a con? "Or do you merely advertise in order to fleece fools of their money, as Charlie seems to think?"

Red-Cloud gifted Charlie with a penetrating glare. "The boy is young. He has yet to learn that not all that is real can be touched or seen with one's eyes.

"I hypnotize people and take them back to where their life took a wrong turn and in doing so, enable them to change its course. I have no idea if that is what you are seeking."

"Can a person really do that?" Charlie shot at Red-Cloud.

"Aye." The Doctor inclined his head. "It has been done."

Vincent turned toward the window to stare into the night. "How?"

"I cannot explain the process. Perhaps it has to do with the shaman blood running in my veins. All I know is that I have the power. I was once a psychiatrist. I used to hypnotize my patients as part of their therapy. One day I discovered that they could actually change their lives by being sent back, and physically making different choices."

Vincent rounded to face him. "What happened? I notice you no longer study psychiatry."

"One of my patients did not come out of her trance and ended up on life support. Unfortunate. I am still unclear as to what happened, but it had to be very traumatic. I was close to disbarment and went through a lot of bad publicity."

"Yet you still practice hypnotism."

The doctor nodded and moved to place a log onto the fire. The wood caught and flames danced and sparked in the grate. After settling into one of the deep velour armchairs, Red-Cloud spoke again. "I gave up my practice to take up the more quiet life of a bookstore owner. Still, I like to keep my hand in with the hypnosis. I have found great joy in assisting the speedy recovery of physical and mental afflictions by using my gift."

"Can you help me?"

"Again. What exactly do you wish? Not to be cursed, or not to be a walking corpse?"

"I want my soul back."

"Good, right answer. Had it been the first, I would not have helped you."

"I thought as much. All I want to do is start my life again, be normal, human, like you and Charlie."

Red-Cloud shot a quick look at Charlie then settled back on Vincent. "Then sit yourself down beneath the tepee and let us begin. Already the hour grows late and this old body of mine grows impatient for its bed."

Vincent shucked off his long leather coat, passed it to Charlie, and crawled beneath the sticks fashioned like a tepee. "Is this completely necessary?"

The doctor took his place opposite. "Aye, that it is, lad. I believe the power in what I do is derived from this wood." He stroked his hand almost reverently down the length of one of the sticks making up the tripod. "This wood has been passed down through my family for many generations. My mother was a Celt and claimed heritage to Merlin himself, and my father was a shaman, as his father and his father before him."

"I thought Merlin was a myth," said Charlie, dropping into one of the armchairs.

Red-Cloud raised a brow. "As were Guinevere, Arthur, and Lancelot I suppose? I only know what my family believes." He turned back to Vincent. "And cannot the same be said about your kind? Are they not just creatures a fiction writer created?"

Vincent gave a half smile. "Point taken."

Red-Cloud grunted in satisfaction. "Then, let us be ready? When you go under, I will come to you, as Vo'ôhma'o, my inner spirit guide. I will lead you. Relax. Close your eyes," he instructed gently in a broad Irish accent. "Imagine a place, a time long ago, where you want to be. Was there a building? What did it look like? Think of the little things that surrounded it. Hear the associated sounds. A song. Someone's voice. Your internal dialogue as well as all of the real, actual, live sounds around you. The more detail you can realize, the more chance we have of success.

"Thirdly, feel. These can be physical sensations or imagined. Can you remember being at the seaside, paddling in a cool ocean? Feeling the sun on your face?"

Vincent felt the moment he lifted. His body weightless. He attempted to open his eyes, but they refused to comply. From what seemed a great distance Red-Cloud's voice sounded in a chant.

He floated on a sea of darkness.

The sensation increased and it was as if he were being pulled along, faster and faster. A pale-blue light appeared in the distance, then a rush of sound like surf. Swept toward the light he was powerless to stop himself. Blinding light flashed in his eyes, then darkness. Stars appeared one by one, and the heavens opened up, then a full moon. Still floating, lush trees and tropical growth below, and the sound and smell of the ocean. He knew this place. Ships bobbed on a tranquil sea, moored in the harbor. He slowed and floated lower to the ground. Two men.

A short, rotund man waited beneath a palm on the beach, as the other, a taller, slighter man strode out of the jungle to meet him.

Lower still Vincent floated.

The taller man spoke, and he knew who he was. "You have work for me?"

The voice so familiar.

"You...you are him?"

"Have you coin?"

The small man took a bag from his inside coat pocket and dropped it into the taller man's hand—into Vincent's hand. He no longer floated, but was a solid being, and his stomach plummeted. He was still a vampire. He had regressed, but not far enough and he knew what was expected of him.

"The mark?" He remembered. He was a man of little words in those days.

"Foch Shanklin."

"His crime?"

The little man rose in height. "He is a murderer and a rapist. He violated my son's wife, then slit my Jonathon's throat. Marianna could not live with the shame and killed herself." The man stopped to swallow, choking back tears. "She was carrying my grandchild."

"And this Foch has gone unpunished? Why?"

"His father is Governor of Port Royal. Foch thinks he lives above the law." The little man stared into Vincent's eyes—a very brave thing to do. He saw and felt his fear.

"Will you see him dead? I would do it myself except...well...I am not a big man..."

"He will not see the morning. Where does he live?"

"With his father, on the edge of town. In the big house with the white columns and a tall, sandstone fence."

Vincent nodded, pocketed the money, and strode into the jungle.

He traveled as the wolf under the cover of darkness until he reached the Governor's abode. The stone fence stood around seven feet tall, but transforming to mist, he floated on the breeze over the fence and through the air until he reached the mansion. He knew he was unable to enter without invitation, so he lingered at each window until he identified which room belonged to the son.

It was not hard, as Foch was in the process of bedding two wenches.

Vincent materialized, hovered outside the window on the ledge, and tapped on the glass.

One of the women looked up and a scream issued from her too-red lips. He ducked out of sight.

Hearing murmured voices, he waited. Footsteps, then the window thrown open and Foch's head appeared. He waved a pistol.

"What the damned..." His eyes widened as Vincent's teeth elongated. His hand shook and the gun discharged.

The bullet went wild, as Vincent grabbed his arm and dragged him toward him. His teeth descended and blood filled his mouth. He held the man fast, and the women screamed. Foch's feeble struggle ceased.

He felt no remorse. The man deserved to die. He had taken three good lives.

He dropped the man back into the room and dissolved to mist...

He floated again, but not as mist. He could feel his body, but not see it. He sped through the dark tunnel, then slowed.

Opening his eyes, he found himself in Red-Cloud's room. Charlie was asleep in an armchair snoring quietly, by the fire. The doctor was watching him.

"I was worried for you," said the old man. "You were gone a very long time. It is almost four in the morning. Did you achieve that which you sought to find?"

"No," he replied quietly, rubbing a hand over the back of his neck. "I did not."

"What happened?"

"I regressed, but not as far as I should have. Something went wrong."

The doctor crawled out from beneath the small tepee, climbed stiffly to his feet, and stretched his limbs. "I regret that you did not get what you came for. Perhaps it was not meant to be."

He came to his feet in one fluid movement. "I do not accept that." Drawing a handful of bills from his pocket, he counted out six one-hundred-dollar notes and held them out to the doctor.

Red-Cloud shook his head as he stared at the money. "I could not. This is way too much."

"I will be back tomorrow night. Call it a down payment."

The doctor took two of the bills and pushed Vincent's hand away. "I will not regress a person more than once. The only time I did...well, that person is still comatose."

"That is a chance I must take. It would be preferable to my present existence."

"Still, I—"

"Please. I am not in the habit of begging." He grasped the doctor's forearm. "I do not ask this lightly."

The doctor pulled away and met his gaze. His eyes almost as deep a blue as he remembered his own to be, it was akin to peering into his soul.

"Very well," the old man agreed. "Ten thirty sharp. We will try one more time, but only once. If we fail—"

"Nine," Vincent cut him off. "And we will not fail." He turned and shook Charlie awake. "Come. We have finished here."

The boy groaned, then sprang awake. "Did I miss something? Did it work? Did you get your soul back?"

"No," Vincent said as he picked up his black leather coat and pushed his arm into the sleeve.

Chapter Nine

Vincent stood over Alara. Her breathing was deep as if no care in the world bothered her. Did she miss him? Did she cry herself to sleep at night whispering his name? She cradled a pillow as she slept, his pillow. Did she imagine it was him? Or did she hate him and despise him for the creature she now knew him to be?

He moved to her dresser and picked up Annabelle's gold locket. It was still here. She had not returned it to evidence. Then his gaze fell to the other item resting beside it and an overwhelming sense of grief overtook him bringing tears to his eyes.

My ring—my father's ring.

He had taken the ring from his father's finger the day he had murdered him. How triumphant and strong he had felt that day, and how shamed all those years later when he had begun to feel and realized what he had done. He had sworn never again to wear that ring, but it was not going to rot in storage, gathering dust for the rest of eternity.

He snatched up the ring and slid it onto his finger.

After all, it was his, his family's legacy. He pushed the ring home, and his vision blurred. In turn he saw his father's face and that of his sister. He staggered, putting his hand to his temple, and turned to come face to face with Alara.

A barrel of a gun leveled at his heart jolted him

back to reality.

"Get out," she enunciated, moving toward him. "Right now. I will count to three. If you are not gone, make no mistake, I *will* shoot."

"A gun cannot hurt me, Alara." His tone was as cold as the gun now pushed snug with his chest. Still, he did not move.

"One."

"I wanted to see you."

"Two." She cocked the gun and her dark-green eyes stared into his, her hand steady. "I have silver bullets."

He raised his hand to stroke her cheek. "I would never hurt you. You know that. Come with me. We could be together. We could be happy."

She drew a deep breath, closed her eyes, then opened them. "Thr…"

He dissolved into a puff of mist and drifted through the crack beneath the window.

****

She stared in disbelief.

She could barely believe what she'd witnessed. She dropped onto her bed and the gun fell from her nerveless fingers to the floor. She covered her eyes with trembling hands. What the hell had happened here? He had been there, right in front of her, then poof, he was gone. She uncovered her eyes and stared at the place he'd stood. Had it been a figment of her imagination? She ran to the dresser. The necklace was still where she'd dropped it. She picked it up and ran her finger lightly over the inscription. *Annabelle Love V.*

What had she been like, her great aunt? Alara had traced the woman as being one of her blood. Annabelle must have been of a stronger caliber than her. Surely, she had known Vincent was a vampire, yet still she had loved him, given her hand in marriage. She wondered, had circumstances been different, and she wasn't the law, would she have succumbed to his charismatic charm and given herself to him wholeheartedly? Could they have been happy as he'd said? Maybe she would become like him...a creature of the night?

"No. Never that," she stated out loud, to reaffirm the words to herself. She shook her head and dropped back onto her bed, her arm across her eyes. She loved the man, yes, but she could never go that far. *Drinking blood.* A shiver of revulsion rushed down her body. *Never.* The thought turned her stomach. Anyway, how did she know he didn't just want her as a replacement for his beloved Annabelle?

She sat again and stared at the window. Yet even now the thought of him had her hot. The sight of him filled her with want, even as she had threatened, even as she had sent him away, made her burn. Alara knew she wouldn't use the gun. She also knew she and Sam would track him down and arrest him for the murder of Lance McManus. However, what did one do with a vampire once they caught one? If they let themselves be caught?

Would it come down to him and her? And what would she do if it did? Would she let him go? Or with Sam by her side, would she find the strength to see her duty through?

And what of Epatha? Something told Alara the vampiress would be a deadly antagonist if cornered.

****

Vincent crossed his arms over his chest and leaned

back against the brick shop wall on the other side of the street and looked up at Alara's bedroom window. The night was brittle cold, but a bright moon shone down. He hadn't expected her to wake. Her light went off, and he imagined her settling back into bed, her breathing even as she drifted into sleep. What had she made of his visit? Had he frightened her? He hadn't meant to frighten her. He just wanted to see her one last time. After tomorrow it would be a moot point anyway. Even should he gain his soul, he must leave this place. He knew he had told Charlie to buy the house, but that was before Alara had discovered his secret. Now, he would disappear again, but he would leave the boy the mansion and a sum of money to keep him in comfort. Charlie had been good to him. He deserved something for his loyalty.

Port Royal had served Vincent well. Perhaps, he would take a trip to the Caribbean. He had money again; it would be easy to disappear. He dissolved to mist but changed his mind and reappeared as the wolf.

It was time he fed, and tonight he wanted real blood.

****

Epatha watched from the shadows as Vincent metamorphosed into his physical body on the footpath beneath Alara's window. Her nails bit into her palms. A curse escaped her lips. She would kill that woman, she swore it. No one took *her* man and lived. Vincent would come back to her. It was only a matter of time. Had he not been pleasant to her at the restaurant? Had he not smiled at her?

She knew deep down he still cared for her, even loved her. They had only to be rid of that skinny bitch,

Alara.

Sweeping her cloak up around her face, she vanished into the night.

****

Sam dragged open the door of the unmarked police car and passed Alara her cup of strong, black coffee, and his cappuccino to hold. He slid into the front seat beside her, and Alara handed his coffee back. "Hope you enjoy it," he said. "I had to walk a block to find an open café. Why didn't I think to pack a thermos?"

"Because you left your last one in the car that got totaled last week, and I haven't got one."

"Oh, yeah, forgot." He nodded toward the building across the road, taking a mouthful of his drink. "Any movement?"

"Yeah, the car went in, but it hasn't come out. I was beginning to think you wouldn't be back in time."

"You sure it's the right car?"

"A light-blue convertible license-plate number, 645REH. It belongs to the boy Charlie's sister."

"How reliable is the hotel clerk?"

Alara slanted him a look. "What's with all the questions?"

"Just want to make sure we don't make any mistakes."

Alara sipped her coffee. "Reliable enough, Armando Pave has no reason to lie. The man's a law-abiding citizen, loyal employee, and has worked at The Edgewater as a desk clerk for fifteen years."

Sam grunted. "And he overheard this conversation how?"

Alara wiped the condensation from her side window and peered across the road at the entrance to the underground parking lot. "After recognizing Vincent from the front page of the newspaper this morning, he listened in on a phone call he put through to Mr. D'Armano's room. Apparently, Vincent was meeting with a Doctor Red-Cloud at nine p.m. The doctor changed the time to eight." Alara frowned. "What would a vampire be doing with a hypnotist?"

"How am I supposed to know? Perhaps he wants to drink his blood."

Her lips thinned. "That's not funny Sam."

"Sorry. Didn't realize you were so touchy."

He slid a glance her way and she turned to stare out the window as tears formed in her eyes.

"You sure you're up to this?" Sam touched her hand. "Up to doing what we might need to do to bring him in?"

She swallowed the lump in her throat and straightened, her resolve hardening. "Of course, I'm up to the job. But there will be no shooting unless totally necessary. Right?"

Sam held his hands up in mock surrender. "Right." He lowered his hands again and took a sip of his coffee. "Now, what do we know about this Red-Cloud person?"

"That's what happens when you take half the day off. You miss out on everything. Where were you anyway?" Her eyes narrowed. "Not at the track. You promised me."

"You were telling me about the doctor," Sam responded with an edge to his tone.

She sighed, gave him a hard look, and peered back out the window. "The only Doctor Red-Cloud I could locate turns out to be an ex-psychiatrist, almost disbarred when he tried to regress one of his patients and she ended up in a coma. Now the doc hypnotizes people privately behind his bookstore on the cheap side of town." Alara took another sip of coffee, then swore and pushed her cup toward Sam, as a blue convertible shot out of the underground parking lot, did a hard right turn in front of them, and headed north. "There they are." She turned the key and slammed her foot on the accelerator. The car roared to life and Sam swore as he almost dropped the coffee.

Keeping a close eye on the taillights of the convertible, and on traffic, Alara followed the convertible into the night, toward what could only end badly for either her or Vincent.

****

A half an hour later, Charlie drew his car to a stop outside Red-Cloud's shop. Vincent was elated when the doctor called to reschedule his appointment. He'd had the shakes all day. Hopefully this time his regression would work properly, and he would gain his soul. He drew his leather coat closer about his neck, not for warmth as he never felt cold, but more for comfort.

He waited for the boy to step from the car and lock the door.

He would miss Charlie's keen wit and sense of humor when he sailed for the Caribbean. The lad had become a good companion. It was a long time since he'd had a friend.

They crossed the road to the store in silence and, this time, Vincent knocked. Three strong raps and the door opened immediately, as if the doctor had waited on the other side.

Red-Cloud led him through to the small sitting

room, leaving Charlie to close the door and follow behind.

The tepee stood in the same place. Not wasting any time, he stripped off his coat, dropped it to the armchair, and climbed through the A-frame to sit cross legged in the tepee.

The doctor followed suit and settled opposite. "You are in a hurry."

"I am eager to begin, yes."

The old doctor studied his face. "You are right of course, but do be aware, it might not work. I must admit, since my failure with the patient on life support, I have not had much success with regression. Perhaps the sticks are losing their magic. They are many hundreds of years old." He straightened his back and folded his hands in front of him. "However, I have been in contact with my father and with your permission, I would like to try something new."

Vincent looked into the old man's deep blue eyes. "Do what you must."

Red-Cloud drew a small leather pouch from his white-fringed shirt pocket.

"What is it?"

"A few dried herbs, no more. To help you relax."

Vincent nodded.

"Put out your tongue."

He frowned, then did as the doctor suggested.

Red-Cloud unraveled the string on the pouch, and poured a small pile of sparkling, rainbow colored powder onto his own palm.

"That looks like no herb of which I know."

The old man remained expressionless. "Trust me."

Once more, Vincent looked into the man's dark

soulful eyes. He could see no malice, so taking a deep breath extended his tongue. The doctor leaned forward and sprinkled a small amount of the powder onto it. The herb tasted bittersweet and dissolved in his mouth with a fizz.

"Swallow," Red-Cloud ordered. Then he drizzled the rest of the sparkling powder down over Vincent's head, to rain over his face and shoulders.

"Shall we begin?"

He nodded. Already he was becoming lightheaded, his thoughts hazing over. Had the old man drugged him? Was this a trap? He could hear Red-Cloud's voice echoing as if at a great distance, chant-like, but could not open his eyes. He tried to move, to get up, but his body was frozen.

"Relax," the doctor soothed. "Think of the place, a time long ago, where you want to be. Was there a certain building? What did it look like? Think of the little things that surrounded it. Sounds. A song. Someone dear to you. Their voice. Your own internal dialogue, and all of the real, actual, live sounds around you.

"Thirdly, feel. These can be actual physical sensations or imagined ones. Touch someone's hand, feel the sun on your face. Grass beneath your feet…"

Vincent was moving, but it was none of his doing. He was being lifted from his body, drawn along. He opened his eyes. He was in a tunnel…intense…dark…

****

Alara slipped from the car into the crisp night air. Black clouds gathered during their drive and light rain sifted down from the heavens. She dragged her coat up close about her body to stop the rain running down her neck and ordered Sam to search around the back of the building. She would take the front.

Approaching the door, she was prepared to pick the lock, something she learned from her days on the streets. But as she touched the door it pushed inward. Alara stilled, thinking it might be a trap. She surveyed the area then stepped inside, the safety on her gun released and ready. Nothing moved. She scanned the darkness with her small flashlight and left the door ajar for Sam.

Creeping across a red patterned carpet toward a brown beaded curtain, she pushed it aside and tiptoed down the narrow hallway. She shut off her flashlight, shoved it into her handbag, and readied her pistol. Then she followed the murmur of voices issuing from a small room up ahead, and the sliver of light beneath the door.

Putting her foot to the door, she kicked. The door crashed back on its hinges, and Charlie sprang to his feet.

Alara leveled the gun at his chest, and the youth raised his hands. But it was not to Charlie to which her eyes strayed. It was to Vincent seated beneath a tepee made of sticks, and the old, Native American dressed in white buckskin, seated opposite him. She presumed the man to be Red-Cloud.

Neither looked at her, and Red-Cloud continued to chant. It was as if Vincent—why did he have to look so good—had not even registered she'd entered. With his eyes closed, his face held the most serene expression she had ever seen on anyone.

"Stop this!" Alara pointed the gun at him.

Charlie took a step forward. "They cannot hear you." He raised one hand in warning. "The doc has

Vincent under hypnosis and he's in some kind of trance himself. It was like this last time."

"Why? How long does it last?"

"Vincent wants his soul back. The doc seems to think he can do it."

"That's ridiculous."

"Vincent doesn't think so."

"Then he's not only a vampire, he's also a fool. And you didn't answer my question. How long will they be like this?"

"Don't know. I fell asleep last time. When I awoke several hours had passed."

"I can't wait that long. I'll have to wake them up."

"How?"

"I can start by pulling this stupid tepee apart." She stepped forward, but Charlie blocked her path.

"You can't do that."

"Get out of my way, Charlie. That's your name, isn't it? As far as I know the only thing you've done wrong is help him. You know nothing of the boy he killed."

"Boy. What boy? What are you talking about? Vincent hasn't killed anyone."

"He's a vampire, Charlie. That's what they do. Kill." She pushed past him and attempted to grab at one of the sticks, but he gripped her arm. They struggled, then as if in slow motion, they were falling.

Alara heard the gun discharge and wondered if she'd shot someone. She crashed into the tepee, colliding with Vincent. Sparkles flew into her eyes, grit filled her mouth, then a tearing sensation, like being drawn along at a terrible speed. She couldn't open her eyes…blackness, thoughts chaotic…and…oblivion…

****

Sam heard a crash and a sound like sticks snapping and burst through the door. It hadn't been locked. He'd checked around back. The only door was bolted from the inside, so he'd decided to come in after Alara.

Another small scream pierced the night.

He raced down the hallway into a sitting room to see three people vanish. He scrubbed at his eyes and pointed his gun at the only body remaining in the room. An old Native American, with gray, plaited hair, and white buckskins, lying prone beside a pile of sticks. As he watched, the old man groaned, rolled over, and directed a stern look at him.

"May the Wise One Above forgive you people for what you have done this night," he stated in a thick brogue.

Sam attempted to help him to his feet, but the old man brushed him aside and rose by himself. He sank into an armchair by the fire, his chest heaving, his hands covering his face.

Sam pointed his gun at the doctor. "What happened here? Where did they go?"

Red-Cloud lowered his hands and looked up at Sam. His eyes were dark, age old, wise. "Put the weapon away, young man. You will get no answers from me with that thing waving in my face." He stood and crouched beside his sticks, picked up one that had been snapped in half, and gently rubbed his hand along the wood. "You stupid, stupid people."

"You didn't answer my question. Where are they?" Sam crouched down beside him. He went to pick up a stick, but quick as a cat, and with strength belying his age, Red-Cloud grasped his wrist.

"Do not touch. Already the sticks have been contaminated. As to what happened here, magic happened here, ancient, and powerful. What was meant for *one,* has now become that for three. May the Wise One have mercy on all their souls."

Sam pushed a hand through his hair. "I don't understand. Where's Alara? What sort of trick is this?"

"No trick, and you don't have to understand. You just have to know it is so."

Sam released a harsh breath and stood. "I suppose if I can believe in vampires, I can believe in magic. So where are they? Where did this magic take them, and can you bring them back?"

"I believe they might be residing in the 1700s. As to, can I bring them back? I do not know. It will not be easy. First there is someone I must contact."

"Then do it." Sam dropped into the armchair and released a harsh breath, then suddenly laughed. "I can't imagine Alara in the 1700s. She must be going insane."

The old man's lips twitched. "I'm certain she will survive, and she has Vincent."

Sam's face darkened. "A damned vampire!"

"If my spell has worked, he is no longer such a creature."

Sam's mind whirled. "What do you mean? You have cured him? Is that possible?"

Red-Cloud met his gaze. "I believe so. Vincent has traveled back to a place he knew before he became a vampire. If he takes the proper steps, he can prevent himself from becoming one of the undead."

"If I had not seen three people disappear, I would say you were mad, but as it is, I am not passing judgment. Just get Alara back."

Red-Cloud raised a shaggy brow. "Just Alara?"

"The other two mean nothing to me."

The old man frowned. "I see." His tone held a hint of censure. He ambled to the door and down the hallway. Sam followed.

Red-Cloud switched on the light in his cozy little bookshop and opened the door onto the street. "Goodnight, Detective Grayson. I would suggest you keep to yourself what you saw here tonight. If you must tell your work something, tell them Alara has taken ill. There are many who do not believe in magic or the paranormal. However, we know different." His smile was eloquent. "Don't we, Sam?"

Sam didn't answer but stepped out into the night. He turned back to Red-Cloud. "How did you know my name? I didn't tell you."

"I know many things." He went to close the door, but Sam's hand shot out to stop him.

"There is another, a female vampire—bad news, be careful. She will come looking for Vincent."

The old man peered across the road as if penetrating the night. "So that is the evil I sense. You best be wary yourself, detective, but thank you for the information. I will be ready." He closed the door before Sam could say more.

Sam squinted and scanned the street both ways. Across the road black shadows cast by the trees in the park appeared like dark sentinels of doom. The hairs on the back of his neck rose and he drew his Glock 19 from his holster, thanking whoever had made the five silver bullets for his gun. With never being a God-fearing man, he said a prayer for the first time in his life.

If Epatha was waiting for him, she wouldn't catch him unaware.

Chapter Ten

Vincent cradled Alara in his arms as she opened her eyes. He brushed the hair back from her eyes. "Are you all right? How did you get here?" he asked gently.

"Vincent, don't worry about her. You have to get out of the sun. There's trees—"

"Let go, Charlie." He brushed at the hand that dragged on his arm. "I am fine."

He frowned. They were in an open field, a low stone fence on one side and several large cypress on the other. The truth was, he *was* fine, but how could that be?

Alara struggled and he released her. He raised his face to the sky and stood, feeling the sun touch his cheeks and eyelids for the first time in over two-hundred years. Whatever Red-Cloud did, had worked.

"Come on, we'll make a run for it." Charlie yanked on his arm.

Vincent grasped Charlie by the sleeves and stared into his eyes. "Charlie, listen to me. I am perfectly all right." He frowned, realizing the truth of those words. Again, he studied his surroundings—a paddock of green wavering grass, haystacks in the distance, a large dam, and across from that…his heart slapped into his ribs…Ashwood, his father's country estate.

He was in Hampshire. England. He was home.

Still in a haze, he spun to stare at the other two.

The old doctor's spell had worked—better than worked, but what about Alara and Charlie? What happened to bring them here?

He tried to help Alara to her feet, but she pushed him away. He frowned. "I cannot understand." He rubbed a hand over the back of his neck. "I sort of know why *I* am here, but what are *you two* doing here?"

Alara scooped her gun from the ground and aimed it at Vincent's chest, and he did a doubletake.

"I am here to arrest you for the murder of Lance McManus. What you might say—"

He began to laugh. "Whoa." He put up his hand, palm out. "How do you suppose you will take me back to the twenty-first century?"

"What?" Alara lowered her gun and looked around. Her bravado seemed to slip, then she raised her pistol and leveled it at his heart. "What are you talking about? Where are we, and how did we get here?"

"I told you not to touch the sticks." Charlie glared at Alara. "Now look what you have done."

"If you hadn't tried to stop me, we wouldn't have fallen."

"Fallen? Fallen where?" Vincent glanced from one to the other.

"Your girlfriend here came crashing into Red-Cloud's place, waving her gun around like a maniac and decided she was going to tear the tepee down around you both. I made a grab to stop her, and she fell pulling me down with her on top of you and here we are." Charlie gave a crooked grin.

"And Red-Cloud? What happened to him?"

"Don't know." Charlie shrugged. "He wasn't here when I woke up, and I was the first to wake."

"You still haven't told me where we are?" Alara waved her gun.

"From my guess, residing in the 1700s. 1700 and what, I am not quite sure, but I am about to find out." Vincent pivoted, ignoring her shouted warning. He heard the gun cock and stopped, but did not turn. "If you are going to shoot, Alara, it will have to be in my back. I have waited for this moment for two-hundred years. I am going home."

****

Alara glowered at his receding back. Home? What did he mean, home? Did he know this place? And what did he mean the 1700s? She tucked her gun into the holster inside her brown leather jacket, hitched her handbag over her shoulder, and raced after him. "What the hell is going on here, Vincent?"

"What do you think is going on here, Alara?" Charlie fell into step beside her, a few paces behind Vincent. "This is Hampshire, England, and that"—he pointed across the small lake—"is Vincent's home."

For the first time she took in the scenery—really looked. Everything smelled so…fresh. Rolling green hills, an expanse of clear blue water, flowers, trees, and an enormous, buff-stone mansion.

She ran the few steps separating her from Vincent and grabbed his arm. "What do you mean home? Is this *your* property?"

He stopped. "It was to be, yes." His eyes were no longer deep pools of ageless time, but a dark blue and his face had a healthy glow of pride. He swept his hand out before him encompassing all in sight. "What you see is Ashwood. My father's country estate. My home. One day to be mine. Is it not beautiful?" He stared up at the sky. "Is the sun not wondrous?" He spun around his arms extended. "Is not all beautiful on God's green earth?" He caught Alara by the waist and twirled her around. "I have arrived home in spring and never again shall I leave!" Still holding her, he planted a hard kiss on her lips.

"Vincent!" Alara gave a half laugh. This was a side of him she had never seen. The playful side. She sobered. There were still too many unanswered questions. "Vincent. Release me!"

He set her down and she staggered back but he caught her, his arms closing around her, molding her to his body, gazing into her eyes. His breath sweet on her face, his lips a breath away. She struggled with the hot wanton sensations the kiss and the close proximity to his warm body evoked. Warm? But—

He set her free and she felt momentarily bereft. "I don't understand any of this." She frowned, eyeing him wearily. "How could this happen? How did we get here, and why are you no longer a vampire?" she asked in an aggrieved tone.

"Magic." He laughed and began walking, his steps long and hurried. "And, what now? Are you upset that I am no longer a vampire? Is there no pleasing you?"

They were rounding the lake of clear blue where black swans glided on a mirror surface with their cygnets.

She stopped. Never had she seen anything so lovely, so free. She realized Vincent had moved on without her and ran to catch up to him and Charlie. The boy was taking everything in with wide-eyed wonder.

"I don't believe in magic," she said at last, falling in alongside them. "There is no such thing."

"The doc said he could do it, and he did it," said Charlie. "What is there not to believe? You are here, aren't you? Explain that if it isn't magic."

Alara conceded and for the first time in her life she was afraid. If she was truly in the 1700s—her hands shook, and she shoved them into her jacket pockets—everything would be different. There would be basically no amenities. Their whole way of life would be different. She was no history major, but she knew that much. She glanced down at her jeans and leather jacket, then at Vincent's black jeans and sweater, and Charlie's cords and windbreaker. "Wait!"

Vincent stopped again and turned back, an impatient look on his dark handsome face. "What is it this time? Please, it has been so long since I saw my home, I—"

"Our clothes. Won't they seem strange to your family?"

****

Family—Vincent stopped in his tracks. If this had worked and he was no longer one of the walking dead, did this mean his family was still alive! His heart slammed into his ribs, and he broke into a sprint. He could hear Alara and Charlie running after him, but he did not stop until he skirted the lake and was behind the cover of a tall conifer hedge, opposite the clothesline out back of the laundry. He waited for the others to join him, then cautioned them to stay while he crept around the edge of the yard keeping close to the high bushes growing on the periphery. He dashed in and grabbed two pairs of breeches, two white linen shirts and a long blue dress.

He turned and sprinted back to Charlie and Alara.

"Quickly, slip into these. We can gather better attire once we reach the house, but these will suffice for now. The servants would not understand the clothes we are wearing."

Alara eyed the gown with distaste. He knew it was enormous, and would most likely drag on the ground, but it was the only dress on the clothesline and most likely belonged to the housekeeper, Mrs. Bosworth, who was no slim maiden. "You can leave your shoes on. The dress will be too long, anyway." He stood waiting for her to move.

"Well?" Alara crossed her arms.

"Well, what?"

"How about turning around?"

Vincent raised a brow. "A little late for that, is it not? I have seen everything you have, and on more than one occasion." He grinned.

Alara flushed, and cast a quick glance at Charlie, but he was already stripping off his cords and wasn't listening. "That was then, this is now," she said, glaring back at Vincent. "We are no longer together. Remember?"

His jaw hardened, and he turned, pulled off his boots, black jeans, and shirt to replace them with too tight breeches and a white shirt that stretched to the max across his wide shoulders. If Mrs. Bosworth was grandiose in size, her husband Samuel, his father's squire, was the opposite.

Vincent struggled to do up the last button on the fly and turned to find Charlie, his clothes fitting perfectly. However, Alara swam in the blue dress. He almost laughed, but the scowl on her face stopped him.

"Give me your clothes. I will stuff them beneath

the conifer hedge and return for them later." He moved away, did as he described, then joined them and held out his arm for Alara to take. "Shall we?"

"Don't be ridiculous." She took a hasty step backward and almost tripped over her dress. "Just get us into the house, so I can dispose of this silly rag."

She hitched up her skirts and tried to step out into the open, but Vincent dragged her back. "Better we take the long way through the garden and enter the side door."

Alara frowned, looking as if she would disagree, then nodded her approval. "You seem to know what you're doing. Lead on."

He led them down the narrow garden path screened by masses of hydrangeas, bluebells, and roses. After following the path for several minutes, it veered left and led to a side entrance.

The mansion was built of buff-colored stone.

Vincent pushed open the carved oak door and stepped into a narrow hallway with a white marble floor, dark paneled walls, and a twelve-foot ceiling. He led the way down the hall lined with ancestral paintings toward a light, which he knew heralded from the five large glass windows. They stepped into the solarium and turned as Alara gasped.

"This is beautiful."

"Yes, it is." He turned to see Alara standing by one of the windows peering out over the lake. She moved from the window to finger a yellow frangipani.

Tropical fauna of every description, several varieties of hibiscus, camellias, frangipani, and more filled the air with the most wondrous perfumed fragrance.

Ferns from the jungle of Peru and India and additional places he could not remember complemented the beautiful blooms.

His mother had loved the solarium. It had been her joy during her illness. Memories crowded his mind, of times he had played here as a child, while she sat reading quietly in her chair by the window. He swallowed down the lump in his throat. "Come. We should keep moving."

He led them from the sunroom down a slightly wider hallway, which opened out into a marble tiled foyer. They were halfway across the antechamber when a huge woman bustled through an adjoining door and stopped at the sight of them.

"Master Vincent." She flushed and pushed a strand of graying black hair from her face. "We were not expecting you today. Your rooms...they are not aired." She glanced at Alara and Charlie and frowned. "You did not send word that you were bringing guests," she added in an aggrieved tone.

"I had a sudden urge to see my father and Abby. These are my friends from the Americas. We met last season in Europe and again in London last night. Mr. Charles Gale and...his sister Miss Alara Gale."

"Mr. Charles, Miss Alara." The woman managed a small curtsy, even as she stared at their strange attire.

"Mrs. Bosworth is our housekeeper," Vincent said throwing the older woman a charming smile. "Her husband, Samuel, has been squire at Ashwood for the past twenty-five years. And I do not know how we would manage without them. Is that not so, Mrs. Bosworth?"

The housekeeper appeared flustered and pushed

another strand of hair back behind her ear. "It is kind of you to say, my lord."

"Now, as you can see, we have run into a mishap and have lost our baggage. We are in dire need of fresh clothing."

"Of course, my lord. Perhaps one of Miss Abigail's dresses might fit Miss Alara, and your father's attire for young Master Charles. He is not so broad as you across the shoulders." She grinned at Charlie, and he flushed, about to open his mouth, but Vincent threw him a hard look and he snapped it closed. It wouldn't do for Charlie to be mouthing any of his American slang right now and setting the servants' tongues to wagging.

"Would you like me to show your guests to their rooms, my lord?"

"No, thank you, Mrs. Bosworth. I will take care of that, but can you send a maid up to air the beds and light the fires? Miss Alara will be staying in the room next to mine, and Master Charles will be in the room opposite."

"I'll see to it, my lordship." The housekeeper lifted her skirts and hastened away.

"Whew! I was too scared to say anything." Charlie wiped the imaginary sweat from his brow. "Wow, is she toffee nosed, or what?"

"Wait until you meet my father." He smiled, elated. His father and sister were alive. He would see Alara and Charlie to their rooms, then track down Mrs. Bosworth and find out when they would arrive home. This had to be a dream. He would pinch himself and wake up and this would all be over, like when he had traveled back to the Indies.

He pinched his leg as he led the way up the grand

staircase to the first floor. It stung like blazes, denoting this was no dream. He grinned at the painting of his Uncle Cedric, third Viscount of Newark, as he passed it by. He never liked the man; today he loved him.

At the top of the stairs, they faced another hall. He stopped at the third door down, opened it, and ushered Charlie inside. "This will be your room. A maid will be up shortly to light a fire and I will be back soon to bring you a change of clothes." Charlie skidded across the polished wooden floor toward the window and spun. "Wow. Can you believe this room? And this bed?" He threw himself onto the blue and cream brocade counterpane of a large four-poster, then rose and dropped into a blue, winged, velvet chair.

"I thought you would like it." He smiled at his young friend and closed the door, leaving Charlie to explore his surroundings. He figured there was enough in the room to keep the boy amused for at least thirty minutes. He crossed the hall to the opposite side, opened the door, and ushered Alara inside. He knew he shouldn't, that the rules of this world dictated otherwise, but he followed her anyway and closed the door behind him. "Are you all right?" He tucked a knuckle beneath her chin and raised her face so that he could see into her eyes. "You have been very quiet since the solarium."

"I...I didn't realize you were so rich."

He sobered. "Is that also a crime?"

She glanced away. "I just feel...so out of my depth." She looked back at him, and he could see a hint of tears in her eyes.

"Do you...do you think we will ever get home again?"

He closed his arms around her and brought her up against his chest, to rest his chin on her hair. Her hair smelled of lavender, and felt like silk, as he knew her body did. She appeared so fragile, his little detective girl, but he knew her to be honed of steel. "You will survive this, Alara. You are strong, and I have a hunch if it is up to Sam, he will be doing all in his power to see you back. Red-Cloud got you here. I am certain he will bring you home. But—" He leaned away and looked down into her face—by God she was beautiful. "Would it be so terrible to stay here with me? We could put everything behind us, start again?"

****

Alara looked into his eyes and all her fear vanished. He was offering himself, forever, always. Isn't that what she had wanted? Vincent not a vampire. Vincent hers to hold and love when she wished? She scanned the room. Could she live here, in this primitive era, without sewage, without electricity? Already shadows were settling and there was no sign of an electric light. A candelabrum stood on the mantel above the hearth and a single candlestick on the bedside table next to a beautifully patterned, porcelain pitcher and bowl. No running water. Then she looked back into Vincent's deep blue eyes and knew she wanted him more than she needed her creature comforts. For, without Vincent, her life would be a dark empty space.

Her hands crept up under his shirt and she felt the warmth of his skin. She stilled. All other times, his flesh had been cold. This time it was hot, scalding hot like the look in his beautiful dark-blue eyes.

Emotion clogged her throat, and she let her eyes speak for her.

Vincent read the message, released a shuddering breath, and bent to touch his lips to hers. "We need each other, you and I. I want you—I love you, and I always will."

"What about Annabelle? You sure I'm not just a substitute for the woman you once loved?"

"Never think that." He hugged her tighter. "I loved Annabelle, yes, but never like this. If you were torn from my arms, I am sure I would die all over again, and this time forever."

"Ssh. No more talk of dying." She closed her eyes and rested her cheek against his heart, which she could feel beating hard and strong in his chest. Why had she not noticed its lack of, before? Blinded by love she supposed.

A moment passed, then he drew back. "I want you to marry me. Will you?"

Her arms slid up around his neck and she ran her hands through his thick dark hair. "When?"

He smiled and his eyes were full of all she had ever wanted to see, love, devotion, forever.

"I can have the banns posted within a week." He let his hands slide down over her hips, caressing the smooth globes of her bottom through her long cotton dress.

"So soon?"

"Would you prefer to wait?" He sounded disappointed, but continued to knead her, then he lifted her to him so she could feel his erection hard against her stomach.

"Just a little longer. Everything is so overwhelming, going so fast. I would like to get to know you better first. The real you. And…" She pushed out of his arms and moved into the room to warm herself at the nonexistent fire. "I would have the answer to this question." She spun. "About nine years ago, in the back room of a drugstore in Seattle, did you find a young colored boy wounded, and did you kill him by drinking his blood?"

All expression dropped from Vincent's face. The color that he had gained from being mortal again drained. He crossed his arms over his chest. "At the time of which you speak, I was holed up in a cabin in Mount Rainier National Park, where I resided for almost ten years, hiding out from Epatha. And yes, to your unasked question. I did kill the boy in the cabin. He was scum, but I did not mean for him to die. I heard him talking to his friend of how he killed an old man and stole his money. Next minute there was a torch shining in my face and a gun leveled at my chest. He fired and I leapt at him. I had starved myself of human blood for ten years. I guess my animal instincts took over. His blood stains my hands. I am not proud of what I did." He spun and walked out of the room, leaving her to stare at a closed door.

Chapter Eleven

Red-Cloud opened his eyes. His warding spell had worked, or she wanted something, very badly. He had fallen asleep in his armchair in front of the fire, waiting. *Stupid.* He should have been dead. He was getting careless in his old age. "Show yourself, lassie. I know you're there."

She was fast, had him by the throat, fangs bared close to his jugular before he could blink. "If you kill me ye will never get him back," he managed to squeeze out.

She released him and moved away, her canines retracting. "Where is he? I saw him come in, followed by *that* woman, and the detective. Only Sam left. Where is he?"

"I presume you are talking about Vincent. I doubt you would be this interested in the boy."

Again, she gripped his throat. "Speak, old man, and I might let you live."

"Gone—back to 1796, if all went well. Unfortunately, the others got caught in the spell."

"You lie." Her grip tightened.

"Why would I?" he asked unblinking, staring into her crimson eyes.

She released him. "You have magic? I could feel the warding spell you cast. Not strong enough to keep Epatha, Queen of the Vampires at bay." She smiled sweetly. "But still impressive. It might have worked on a lesser creature." She drifted toward the mantel to study a small glass figurine of a cat. "From where does your magic stem?" She didn't turn.

He watched her closely, ready for another sudden attack. "Mostly from that pile of broken sticks on the floor."

Her gaze shifted to the sticks scattered on the bearskin rug, as he moved to put a log on the fire. She stepped aside. He was safe for the time being; he knew that. She needed him, and until such a time as she didn't deem him necessary, his life would be preserved. That gave him a small measure of time to figure out how to be rid of her.

"So, what do ye want?" He stood and faced her. She was definitely a beautiful woman. Her eyes reverted to aquamarine as he watched, a vulturous body, blue-black hair, and a sultry pout to her lips. No wonder Vincent had once succumbed. "I mean, ye must want something, or I would already be dead."

"I need you to send me back."

Red-Cloud frowned and bent to place the log into the hearth, then climbed slowly to his feet. He stood with his back to the fire. However, it was unable to take the chill from his body her words evoked. Could he do it? Could he send her back? And could he take the responsibility for unleashing her on Vincent once more. "It was an accident. I have no idea how it happened. I am not sure—"

She was on him so fast he barely had time to blink. Grasping his throat with one hand, she lifted him effortlessly to dangle his feet above the floor. "You better be certain. Your life depends on your certainty."

Epatha was slight, but her strength was prodigious, and she was dangerous, very dangerous. He required time to think. "The sticks. I will need to—"

She dropped him and turned as if he was nothing, and he fell heavily to the floor, pain shooting through his arthritic knees.

"I have to mend the sticks." He gasped, craning his neck to look at her. She moved to stand before him, her face a mask of evil beauty.

"Tomorrow night at eight. And no tricks." She swept her cloak up around her face and dissolved to mist, and he watched her squeeze through the crack beneath the closed window.

Red-Cloud wondered how she'd managed to gain entry. She had not been invited. But perhaps, to one of her power, an invitation was unnecessary.

****

Vincent strode down the marble hallway. After his confrontation with Alara he needed to let off steam. He'd gone to his old room, changed into his riding attire, collected clothes for Charlie from his father's room, delivered them, then found his way to the stables. His stallion, Tornado was in his stall, and he'd saddled the beast without calling the groom.

With the wind in his face and the clean country air of this era in his lungs, his mind soon cleared. He supposed Alara had her reasons for asking. The person she spoke of must have played a significant part in her life, but why had she chosen that moment to ask? Why did she have to have such suspicion in her voice?

He thought they were past suspicion and hostility now that he had become human again. He wanted nothing more but to forget all those years of blood and torture, the dark shadow on his spirit. Epatha must be responsible for Alara's friend's death for he certainly knew nothing about it.

He had his soul back. He must have. He lifted his face once more to the sun and it reached down and touched him with its warm English heat, and his heart beat strong in his chest. And he felt whole again.

He finished his ride in higher spirits and decided it was time to familiarize himself with his old house. He had Alara and Charlie to care for now, so he would be taking on a larger role in the running of the estate. Something his father had always wished him to do.

He stopped at his father's study, pushed open the door, and stepped inside. It still held the same familiar scents of spicy cologne, pipe tobacco, and old books. His mother's portrait hung pride of place above the wide hearth. Raven hair, deep blue eyes, and her skin, porcelain pale. In a gown of blue satin and gold brocade, she was still the most beautiful woman he had ever looked upon. He reached up to touch the hand in the painting. He had been eight when they'd moved from Venice to settle in England. Ten when she died giving birth to Abigail. His mother being of noble English birth had wanted an English education for her son. He attended and graduated from Oxford.

Vincent strode across the navy patterned rug and ran his hand over the polished walnut and olivewood desk, his mind drifting back to that last fateful day...

He had found his father behind this desk hard at work on the books.

He pushed the thought from his mind, turned, and strode from the room.

Heading toward the stairs, he was about to pass the

mail table when he noted a copy of the London Times and was jolted back to reality by the date on the front page. August 2, 1796. He snatched the paper from the tray. "Hell's bells!" The same day he had returned from Europe. Four days before Epatha had made him. Clutching the newspaper tightly in his fist, he marched in search of Mrs. Bosworth.

He located the housekeeper in the kitchen arguing with the cook.

"How old is this?" he demanded, thrusting the newspaper before her face. "When did it arrive?"

"Why, just this morning, my lord. I do believe it is yesterdays. Is there a problem?"

Vincent frowned. "No." He realized his behavior would be regarded as irrational had he said more. "No, nothing is wrong." He took a deep breath, about to turn away then swung back. "My father, when is he expected?"

"Why, this evening, my lord. He has taken Miss Abigail into the village to pick up her new spring wardrobe from the seamstress. Is there anything I can help you with?"

Vincent forced a smile. "No. That will be all, thank you, Mrs. Bosworth." He hastened out of the room.

****

Alara stared into the gilt-edged mirror on the Louis XV dressing table. She was certain she'd been cast in a scene from *Alice Through the Looking Glass* and a white rabbit would pop out at her at any moment.

A maid stood behind her, torturing her tangle of short blonde curls into a semblance of order with a hot curling iron.

Mary had arrived about five minutes after

189

Vincent's departure.

Alara, racing to the door to call him back after their argument, had come face to face with the girl carrying what the maid explained was a day dress over her arm. Then on discovering Alara's lack of proper foundation garments, Mary had hurried away again only to return with what Alara termed in her mind a torture device. After being pushed, prodded, and coaxed into a pale blue and white corset, and helped into the day dress, Alara now sat staring dumbfounded into the mirror at the stranger she had become.

She prayed for deliverance.

Her prayers were answered when a knock sounded, and Charlie poked his head around the edge of the door. "I wasn't sure, but I thought this was your room." He smiled at the maid, and she flushed and gifted him with a small curtsy.

"Come in, Charlie, we're finished here."

"But, Miss Alara, we—"

"You can complete doing my hair later, Mary. I would like a private word with my brother." Her tone brooked no argument.

"Very well, miss." The girl gave a small bob and headed for the open door, throwing Charlie another flirtatious smile as she passed.

Alara waited for the girl to close the door before rising. She took a couple of deep breaths. She couldn't believe she was wearing stays. She moved toward Charlie, who was resplendent in buff-colored breeches, pale hose, gold satin waistcoat, and burgundy jacket.

She sank onto the edge of her four-poster. "I think you made an impression."

"Do you think?" Charlie flashed an engaging grin.

"She was cute."

"I'm certain they have rules about fraternizing with the servants here."

His face fell. "Pity. I could've got her to tie this thing." He pulled what looked like a lacy scarf from his pocket and shook it out.

"I think that's called a cravat. I've seen them in old pictures, but I've no idea what to do with it." She turned to look out the window into the darkness. "Have you seen Vincent?"

"Not since he tossed some clothes into my room earlier. Guess he's catching up with people and stuff."

There was a tap at the door and Charlie spun and pulled it open. "Speak, and he shall appear." He grinned and gave a small bow.

Vincent stepped into the room and Alara noted the newspaper in his hand.

"You look lovely," he said, eyeing her up and down. "The lemon suits you." The look in his eyes told her he had forgiven her, and more.

"I'm wearing stays," she blurted, then could have bitten out her tongue.

"Are you indeed?" He gave a half laugh.

"I'm sorry. I should have known you were innocent, but I had to hear it from your lips."

Vincent took her hand and dropped a kiss into her palm. "And I should not have left you like that. This place is strange to you. I am afraid my etiquette is almost nonexistent after so many years away."

Charlie coughed softly from behind them. "Perhaps I should leave."

Vincent spun, as if seeing Charlie for the first time. "Forgive me. No, you should stay." He held up the rolled newspaper. "I know now what I have to do. Have you any idea of the date?"

"I'd imagine somewhere in the 1700s," replied Alara, watching him, an uneasy feeling in her stomach.

"The third day of August 1796."

"And that has significance, why?"

"It is precisely four days before Epatha made me. The day I arrived back in London from my European sabbatical."

"And?"

"And that is where my other self will be. At my father's townhouse."

"What do you mean, other self?" Alara asked, frowning.

"Red-Cloud sent him back to save his soul." Charlie stood at the open fire warming his hands. "He hasn't done it yet."

Vincent nodded. "The last time the doctor hypnotized me, I appeared in some kind of spirit form, and on seeing my other self, I merged with his body. This time my whole body has been sent back. Whether the doctor intended it that way, or whether it had something to do with you two falling onto his tepee, I don't know. All I know is that I'm here, and somewhere in London—"

"There is another you," finished Alara.

"Unaware of what is about to happen to him," added Charlie.

"Precisely." Vincent nodded. "That is why we have to kill Epatha."

"What!" Charlie's voice rose.

"You're insane." Alara shook her head.

"That may be so, but it is the only way to stop her.

However, I want to see my father and sister first. They will be home this evening. I would like to spend at least a couple more days here, then we will travel to London."

Alara sank onto the bed, his words flittering through her mind as she stared into space. His father and sister were alive. He must be so pleased. Of course, he would want to see them.

Then, London—London 1796—what would it be like? She heaved a breath, unable to imagine. She got up and began to pace. She would survive. Of course, she would survive. She was tough; she had been brought up tough. This was just another one of life's ordeals, which she would overcome. She raised her chin and looked at Vincent, handsome, tall, proud, proud of his home, proud to be alive again, strong. She scooped her handbag from where she'd kicked it under the bed when the maid arrived, pulled out her gun, and snapped it open. Five silver bullets stared back at her from their housing. "I have these," she said, holding the gun out for Vincent to see.

He met her gaze. "They were meant for me. The ones you threatened me with that night in your room."

"Merely a deterrent, but had it come to it, yes, I might have used them. People were getting murdered, Vincent. I had no idea until a few days ago whether you or Epatha or both of you were responsible."

He took the gun, closed it, and handed it back to her. He cupped her cheek. "You keep it. I would have my lady safe. I know Epatha. I know how to handle her, and don't forget I have been in the predicament she will place me in, once before. This time I will be ready. Now…" He smiled at Charlie and took the crumpled cravat from his hand. "I will give you a lesson in tying the most important item in a young gentleman's wardrobe."

****

Alara dismissed her maid and stared into the mirror. Was that young lady with tiny white flowers threaded through her hair, in the low-cut blue and gold brocade gown, really her? She put her hand to the heavy jeweled necklace at her throat. Vincent had sent the sapphires and the gown to her via the maid, with a note attached. Both items had belonged to his mother, and he would be honored should she deem to wear them to dinner.

Alara had never seen anything more beautiful in her life, and the thought of how much the sapphire and diamond necklace cost made her stomach queasy. She rose from her seat at the dresser and hastened across the room to throw open the window shutters. She gulped in several large mouthfuls of fresh evening air and put a hand to her stomach. She really did feel ill. Nerves, she imagined, at the prospect of meeting Vincent's father and sister for the first time.

A knock sounded at the door. She drew a deep breath and spun, and another bout of nausea overtook her. Vincent poked his head around the edge of the door." Ready?"

She swallowed the bile that rose to her throat and forced a smile. "As ever."

He frowned and crossed the floor. Gently grasping her shoulders, he looked down into her face. "Are you ill? You are the color of tallow. Should I summon the doctor? Are you too hot in that dress, or not warm enough?" he asked, chaffing her arms. "I'll have a shawl brought, and your fire needs stoking." He went to move toward the fire, but she grabbed his arm.

"Don't be silly. If anything, I'm hot. I'm just hungry." However, in reality, food was the last thing on her mind. They had eaten a light lunch of cold mutton, bread, and a thick vegetable soup after their meeting several hours ago. Now just the thought of food made her stomach squirm. "I'm sure it's only nerves at the prospect of meeting your family, and coffee withdrawals." There. She brightened. She'd hit on it. "I was a bit of an addict."

"If you're certain, then…and I will see if we can locate some coffee."

"Don't fuss." She held out her hand. "I'll survive."

He took her hand and drew her into his arms. "You look beautiful. The blue suits you. When this is all over with Epatha, I will have a gown of every color sewn for you."

"Do you think we can defeat her?" Alara's stomach clenched.

"She is very old and extremely dangerous, but with the three of us, I am in no doubt."

She forced a smile and hugged him a little tighter. Had she only just gained him as a man, to lose him again? She wished she felt as certain as he sounded.

****

The table in the dining room ran at least ten feet long and wrought of dark polished wood. Beautiful, as was all the furniture in Vincent's father's house. Two large candelabra sat at different intervals along the table and another two, on sideboards against the wall. A large blaze burned in the hearth and in the warm glow of the candle and firelight, Alara picked out the silhouette of a

195

man at the other end of the table. The figure rose and walked toward them as she and Vincent moved farther into the room.

"Father, may I present, Miss. Alara Gale. I see you have already met Charles."

His father, a tall, distinguished man with steel-gray hair tied back in a ponytail, raised a dark brow. When he spoke, his words held a slight Italian accent. "A most unusual young man." Lord D'Armano took Alara's hand and gave a brief bow, then he touched his lips to her fingers and released her. "Delighted to meet you, Miss Gale."

"Please, call me Alara." She smiled. He seemed very charming, and not at all the ogre Vincent had hinted at.

"You may call me Leland." His lips curved as he returned her smile. "Your brother tells me you are from the Americas. Fascinating. You must educate me more on your country. Do they really have red men there?"

"Later, Father." Vincent led Alara halfway down the table, pulled out the seat opposite Charlie, and waited for her to sit. At first slightly flustered, she then realized what was intended, and hurriedly sat. Vincent then strode to the other end of the table. He had just settled when a young girl of about sixteen rushed into the room. With face flushed, emerald eyes glowing with excitement, and masses of dark red hair swirling about the shoulders of her pale-pink high-necked gown, she threw herself into Vincent's arms. He rose to catch her, twirled her around, and dropped a kiss on top of her head before steadying her. She kept her arm about his waist.

"Vincent, I am so happy to see you." She was all

smiles. "You must tell me about your travels. Is it true that you brought home two Americans, and they were half naked?"

Vincent laughed softly. "Perhaps, you can see for yourself, poppet." Taking her by the shoulders, he turned her to face down the table.

Seeing Alara and Charlie, she slapped a hand to her mouth.

"I have done it again, have I not?" Her bright gaze flew to her father. "Papa is always telling me I engage my mouth before my brain. I am so sorry. Please, forgive me. I am just excited to see my brother. He has been away simply forever—almost two years." She spun and faced Vincent. "Did you bring me a present?" She clasped her hands. "You promised you would."

"And so, I did, but unfortunately we were set upon by highwaymen not three miles from here and all our baggage stolen." Vincent took his seat and his sister flopped down into the seat beside him. He threw a desperate look at Alara. She knew he'd lied, but she supposed he had to explain their lack of clothing somehow.

"Those horrible men, to steal my present." Abigail pouted. "Papa, you must track them down and hang them."

"I will have the sheriff summoned come morning," Lord D'Armano placated, taking a sip of red wine. "I fear for our lives every time we set forth from our house. Those men are barbarians."

Vincent nodded. "I have already informed the sheriff of the incident. However, I feel it is of little use, as our thieves are likely halfway to London by now."

"I will make certain the driver is armed when we

travel to London tomorrow." Leland signaled to the butler to refill his glass as several maids walked into the room with soup bowls. Alara watched to see what the others would do, and when she saw Abigail lift her spoon to eat, she followed suit. Peering across the table, she noticed Charlie did the same. She smiled her encouragement, and he gave her one of his engaging grins. He seemed to be adapting to his new surroundings with little trouble.

"You are going to London?" questioned Vincent, taking a small white roll from the basket on the table.

"Your sister is being introduced into society, have you forgotten? I did write you on the subject."

"Of course. A friend of Mama's, was it not?"

"Lady Pottaby, who was a great friend of Mama's and is sister to the wife of the Earl of St. Audries, has offered to sponsor me." Abigail gushed. "Is that not exciting? Papa is escorting me to London to pick up my coming out gown, and we are to take tea with Lady Pottaby at two o'clock. She has arranged so many outings. Papa says I am certain to snare a wealthy husband in no time at all."

Lord D'Armano made a small choking sound. "Not if you do not learn to curb your tongue, you will not. Remember, young ladies of station should not always say what is on their mind. I thought we spoke on this subject this morning."

"Yes, Papa." Abigail bowed her head, but Alara could see a smile on her lips.

"Will you and your friends not join us in London, Vincent?"

"Perhaps in a few days. I would show Alara and Charles Ashwood first, and I have promised to take

Alara riding."

Had he? It was the first Alara had heard of it. She had never been on a horse in her life and was not particularly fond of the creatures since she'd been bitten when visiting a traveling carnival as a child. However, she kept her silence, thinking it more prudent to listen than speak as five more servants moved into the room, collected the bowls, and set down several large platters of jellied meats, roast pheasant, smoked trout, venison pie, and a bowl of hot potatoes in melted butter.

Alara's stomach heaved. It would be a miracle if she got through this dinner without losing the contents of her stomach. Her heavy gown and tight foundation garments were only adding to her dilemma.

"I will see you in London on the seventh, then. Lady Pottaby has planned Abigail's coming out ball for the twentieth. I am certain Alara will have a wardrobe to see to as her clothes were thieved." Leland peered along the table at her and frowned. "Are you well, my dear? You look pale. Or is it the shadows from the candlelight?"

Alara took a sip of wine and forced a nod. "I am well, my lord."

"And a wedding dress to order." Vincent said, giving Alara a steady look. "Alara has consented to be my wife, although we have not set a date as yet."

"How exciting!" Abby clapped her hands. "You must allow me to help choose the fabric, Alara."

"Of course." Vincent had to bring up the wedding now when she was feeling ill. She smiled her acceptance.

Charlie came from his chair, strode the length of the table, and slapped Vincent on the back. "Well done, man. 'Bout fucking time." Abby and Count D'Armano stared at him open mouthed, and Charlie, realizing what he'd just done, apologized. He gave two quick bows. "Forgive me, your lordship." He turned back to Vincent. "I mean congratulations, hope you and Alara will be very happy."

Vincent laughed and shook his hand. "Thank you, Charlie. I am certain we will be extremely happy. They have a strange way of speaking in America," Vincent noted to his father. "It does take a bit of getting used to."

Charlie grinned at Lord D'Armano. "Vincent has been trying to teach me your language, sir, but I'm afraid I'm failing miserably."

The boy returned to his seat, threw Alara a helpless glance, reached for his glass of wine, and downed it in several swallows.

"If anything, Vincent has picked up your accent. His Italian and English are almost indistinguishable." Leland's tone hardened. "Once you are wed, I hope you will be less inclined to wander."

"I can assure you, Father, my traveling days are over. I can think of nothing more enchanting than settling down with Alara and raising a small brood of grandchildren just for you." Vincent winked at Alara, and she smiled back thinly.

The mountain of rich food, the thought of marriage and children while she was trying to resign herself to living in 1796, and the pressure of acting like something she wasn't was all becoming a little unbearable.

The maids trailed into the room to collect the empty plates. She had barely touched hers. They set down two hot puddings and a heaped plate of sweet tarts, and Alara's stomach did a final lurch. She bounded to her feet and fled.

Chapter Twelve

Sam stood behind the door in Red-Cloud's sitting room and checked the round of silver bullets in his gun. The clock on the mantel ticked away the minutes, and a drop of perspiration marked a path down his spine. Red-Cloud sat silently alert in a deep armchair next to the fire and straightened even more as a puff of mist squeezed through the crack beneath the window and materialized at the center of the room.

"Don't move," Sam growled, his pistol aimed at her heart, "or you are dead. I'm taking you in for murder."

Epatha laughed. "Fool. Do you really think to hurt me with that toy?"

"This gun has silver bullets."

"Does it just?" Her canines extended and before he could blink, she was on him. A shot discharged. Epatha staggered, then came at him again, seemingly undaunted.

And again, he fired. She stumbled, then grabbed his gun hand, her strength prodigious. She forced the pistol around to point at his heart and stared him straight in the eye.

Her eyes burned red in a pale mask of beauty. Teeth, long, pointed, and evil, spiked from her gums. Sam knew he was dead.

But she staggered.

In a haze of pain from fingers clamped around his throat, he saw Red-Cloud's face behind her, and in his hand, a carved granite bookend.

Epatha snarled and flung her arm wide, striking the old man across the head. He fell to the ground.

The gun went off and Sam's shoulder burned. He looked down. Red stained his shirt. Epatha wrenched the gun from his hand and flung it at the bookcase. Then she picked him up as if he were nothing, and her mouth descended.

"Wait!" Red-Cloud's voice rang out. "If you kill him, I will never send you back!"

Epatha snarled low in her throat, eyed Red-Cloud for a split second, then hurled Sam to follow the gun into the bookcase. He fell hard. The bookcase rocked and sent books tumbling down around him. His hands were little protection as two large volumes struck his head and wounded shoulder, sending stars blazing before his eyes. Another book caught him in the temple. Then the whole bookcase crashed down, and his world went black...

****

Epatha dragged Red-Cloud up by the scruff of his neck and dropped him into an armchair. She removed her necklace and held the red stone to the wound in her breast. The pain burned with the intensity of fire, but she had been made by the *Maker* himself and inherited his magic. She could not be killed by ordinary means as her life-force was contained within the jewel.

The pain intensified, then slowly she felt a movement as she watched the bullet work its way to the surface and pop free of her flesh to drop onto the rug, all pain dissipating. She repeated the procedure with the wound in her shoulder, then refastened her necklace and faced the doctor who was staring on in fascination.

"Now, where were we? Oh yes!" She smoothed down the sides of her long red gown. "You are going to send me back to find Vincent, or I will rip out Sam's heart while you watch. Then I will—and make no mistake, I am able to prolong my victim's deaths for several hours—kill you, *slowly*." She dragged Red-Cloud from his chair. "Ready?"

The old man struggled to break free. "The Wise Ones will punish you for this, make no mistake. No one can live forever, not even you."

"Shut up! And get under there." Epatha pushed him toward the mended tepee and followed him down to sit opposite. The last thing she needed was him spouting on about his gods. Didn't he know she was immortal? She feared no god.

"Remember, any false moves and both of you die."

"How do I know he is not already dead?" Red-Cloud looked over at Sam.

"I can hear his heart beating, and the blood pounding in his veins, albeit slowly." Her lips curved in a cold smile. "Perhaps you should hurry. Also, if you intend to trick me and send me somewhere other than where I wish to go, I will hunt down every one of your ancestors and take their souls."

"Ye wouldn't."

"I do not make idle threats."

Red-Cloud nodded in resignation and drew a pouch from his pocket. He poured a small amount of the sparkling contents out onto his palm then leaned forward to sprinkle it over her head, but she gripped his arm. His bones felt weak and fragile beneath her fingers. Mortals, they were such weak creatures. "What is it? This powder you sprinkle?"

"Magic powder. You must trust me if this is to work." He stared deep into her eyes, and it took all her willpower to break his hold. The old devil was more powerful than she imagined.

She looked away and released him. "Very well, but this better not be a trick."

Red-Cloud tried again and this time he sprinkled the powder down over her hair, and it fell about her shoulders and face like silver rain.

"Now hold out your hand."

Epatha hesitated but did as he asked, and he poured a little more powder onto her palm.

"You must sample it. That is what Vincent did. I saw it fall upon his lips and he licked them."

She poked the tip of her tongue into the powder and drew it into her mouth. It was not at all gritty but seemed to dissolve with a fizz and tasted bittersweet.

He held up his hand. "Now stare at my ring and think of the place where you would like to be. Of sounds associated with the place, the smell of the air…"

She stared at the golden ring on his finger, and her mind filtered back. Where would Vincent be? Where would he go? She smiled. Of course, where would anyone go that had been away so long…home. He would go home to Ashwood.

She stared at the ring, and it filled her vision. There was a sensation of floating at an appalling rate, but she couldn't move. Darkness, then swirling colors, an intolerable ringing in her ears, an ache in her head and black, then a pinpoint of light. She cried out as pain clawed at her insides. Was this a trick? Then…blessed oblivion…

****

Vincent boosted Alara onto a side-saddle on the back of a small gray gelding he called Caesar. Apparently, the animal was the gentlest horse in the stable and was trained to stop should his passenger begin to fall. Caesar belonged to Abigail, and it was she who had insisted Alara ride him.

How Vincent had convinced her to do so, Alara still wondered. She was still lightheaded from her ordeal last night. Or was it nerves from being on horseback for the first time?

She gripped the reins tighter and forced a smile when he asked if she was well. She wondered if she should even ride while she was pregnant. Was it safe for the baby, and just how far along was she?

She nodded and watched Vincent mount his tall black stallion with ease and sit tall in the saddle. The animal danced to the side, but he brought him firmly under control after a quiet word in the animal's ear. With a reassuring smile at her, he led the way out of the stable at a sedate walk.

Two hours later, after an enjoyable first riding lesson, Vincent drew his horse to a halt beside the lake and lifted Alara from her saddle. She found solid ground on shaky legs and steadied herself by grasping Vincent's hands. His arms tightened around her waist and held her—just held her, safe, secure, just where she wanted to be.

He leaned back and his lips brushed the tip of her nose. "How are you feeling? I was worried about you last night. You sure you are not ill?"

She nodded. "Just a little unsteady from my first

horse ride, but it wasn't the ordeal I thought it would be. In fact, it was quite enjoyable." She broke loose and settled on the grass by the water, wondering how she would tell Vincent she was pregnant.

He sank down beside her, encircling her waist and brought her up close against him. "It is beautiful here. I never want to leave. I cannot believe how I took this place for granted." He dropped a small kiss on her forehead. "And it is even more special because you are here with me." He lay back on the lush grass with his hands beneath his head, staring up at the cloudless blue sky." You don't have to say anything. I know you feel out of place here." He sat up again and brought her back into his arms. "You were always so strong. Now you seem so fragile, as if you would break. Forgive me. I know I have done this to you." He stroked her hair. "If there is anything I can do to help you adjust, you know I would do it. Even if it meant…letting you go."

Alara turned in his arms and came up to her knees, cupping his cheeks with her hands. His words were so heartfelt, so unsure. Had she done this to him, her strong vampire lover? "Don't say that. I never want you to let me go. You are everything to me. The air I breathe, the beat of my heart. Do you know how close I was back in our time to throwing all caution out the door and running to you? It broke my heart that night you walked away from me."

His answer came not in words, but in actions. His fingers traced a path the length of her throat, and down her arm. She shivered, but not from the cold. When his hand cradled her breast through her riding habit, she drew in a sharp breath, but didn't pull away. Hot blood coursed through her, setting her body aflame. She continued to stare into his dark-blue eyes and felt as if she were drowning in them. She moistened her lips with the tip of her tongue, and slowly, ever so slowly, he leaned toward her. His mouth grazed hers with agonizing tenderness. A yearning cried out from deep within her soul, begging to be quenched. It had been so long since he'd really touched her, since they'd made love. She felt a tear trickle down her cheek and cursed herself for being a fool. Why was she getting so emotional?

His lips touched hers again, ever so gently, and she could barely breathe. How could she love him so much, yet how could she not? With a primal growl low in her throat, her fingers twisted through his shaggy black hair, and in one skillful movement he turned her to lie on her back and came down over her.

"What makes me think you have done that before?" she said, looking up at him.

"Long ago in another lifetime, maybe, but never again except with you."

"Right answer." With her hand behind his head, she drew his mouth down to hers. Her tongue played lightly over his lips for a moment, then his lips took hers, hungrily, drinking deeply of her kiss. He kissed her with such desperate need, such urgency, as if they were two souls wrenched apart and he was determined to entwine them once more.

What they'd shared before had been powerful, but nothing had touched on this. He leaned back and stripped off his coat and shirt, and his burnished muscles rippled beneath the sun. This was Vincent, the real Vincent, not the pale man he'd become. She raised her hand to touch his chest, and his heat struck her.

He helped her off with her riding jacket and unfastened her shirt, slipping it from her shoulders. She had deliberately taken off her corset and wore only her black bra which she had on the day they'd been sent back. His hand found her breast and his thumb grazed over her sensitized nipple, and again his warm skilled lips and his bold delicious tongue found hers.

The fastening on her bra melted away and the feel of his hard satiny chest against hers was pure heaven. His desire strained against his breeches, branding her with his heat. When his large firm hands slid down her spine and cupped her buttocks nestling her close to his hard erection, she thought she would die of pleasure.

Alara reached for the buttons on Vincent's pants and flicked them open. He moved back to discard them and helped her off with her skirt. Only her black panties remained, and they were no hindrance to his deft fingers.

For a moment he knelt looking at her, feasting on her with his eyes, then he came down over her, covering her body.

****

Vincent was afire. He could barely contain the furor that burned within him and the way Alara writhed as he tongued her taut pink nipples made him worse. She pressed her hand to his nape to hold his head in place as he sucked greedily at each breast in turn, wrenching soft groans from her throat.

A moment later, he rolled her over bringing her lush nakedness down on top of him. He wanted to see her lovely green eyes staring into his, filled with desire. His fingers caught her nape, and he brought her head down for another drowning kiss. The way she responded—trembling against him, opening her mouth wide to his passionate possession—stirred him unbearably.

She threaded a hand between their bodies, touching him, tearing from him a delighted groan. She stilled for a moment, then slowly caressed him again, ever so skillfully.

Unable to take any more, he turned her and stroked her mound of curls with his fingers. He slid a finger inside her, felt how slick and snug she was, and gazed into her fevered eyes. He removed his finger and thrust into her.

She gasped and he brought his lips down over hers, moving gently within her, but when she sucked his tongue inside her mouth, his passion broke free. His kiss smothered her moans as he plunged faster, over and over, surging higher and harder, until he felt her body explode around him. He heard her sigh, and she melted into his final deep thrust as he shuddered inside her. He collapsed to the side holding her close, his heart pounding, his breathing labored.

Together they lay in silence, quietly as one, until finally he rolled over to brush her hair back from her closed eyes and stroke her cheek. "How do you feel?"

She opened her eyes. "A bit tender."

"Sorry." He dropped a kiss onto her nose.

"Don't be." She raised her arms to encircle his neck.

"Not about that."

"Then what?"

"I didn't use any precautions. As a vampire I had no reason to. Vampires can sire no children."

Alara pushed away, climbed to her feet, and pulled

on her skirt. "I think you are wrong about that." She picked up her bra and fastened it.

Vincent sprang to his feet. "What are you saying?" He grasped her arms, his grip tightening as his face darkened.

"That I'm pretty certain I'm pregnant." She tried to break his grip. "You are hurting me."

He shoved her away and dragged on his breeches. "Impossible."

"Then whose?" She watched him, his back stiffening as she spoke. "I haven't been with anyone but you in three years."

He threw her a look that spoke volumes and if looks could spear, she would be dead. He snatched up his shirt and dragged it over his head, then pushed his arms into his coat sleeves. His movements, furious. "Get dressed. It is getting late, and a storm is brewing."

****

A storm all right. Alara watched him. His dark expression was thunder itself. She finished dressing with a hurtful lump in her throat. She strode over to her horse and attempted to mount, but when she was unable to manage, begrudgingly allowed him to help. He did so in cold silence.

Of all the things she expected it was not disbelief and mistrust. At her first realization last night that she was pregnant, she felt upset. Then after contemplation, she'd become resigned, even a little excited. She thought Vincent would be happy. He had spoken of children to his father. They were to be married. How had she known vampires couldn't sire children? It wasn't as if she'd read up on the subject.

She'd felt sick almost from the moment she'd

awoken in the back paddock and had grown continuously worse each day. Her cycle should have occurred the day they arrived. It hadn't, and the only thing she could deduce was that she was pregnant. It had to be something to do with them traveling back in time and Vincent no longer being a vampire. It was the only explanation, however unbelievable. And now, Vincent didn't believe her. That hurt most of all. He thought her unfaithful. That was just wonderful. Stuck in 1796, pregnant, and for all she knew, the way he was treating her, soon to be homeless. She could barely look at him as he mounted his horse and asked if she was ready to leave. She nodded. How could he be so unreasonable? How could he think so little of her? She slapped her reins to her horse's neck, sending it cantering toward Ashwood, leaving him to follow behind. She just hoped she didn't break her neck on the way back, or perhaps, that could be the answer to all her problems.

****

Vincent arrived back in the stable to find Alara dismounting. "Don't be a little fool, wait for me to help you."

"I can do it myself."

She twisted in the saddle, removed her foot from the stirrup, and attempted to slip from the horse, but her skirt became entangled. Vincent dismounted and rushed toward her, just in time to catch her before she fell face first. She struggled in his arms and tried to tear her skirt free, but his arms tightened around her.

"Hush and let me untangle you."

"I don't need help from someone who thinks I'm a liar!" She fought against him, yanked at the skirt, and heard it tear. "Now look what you've done." She stilled, looking down at the hole in Abigail's riding habit. Tears welled in her eyes.

"Are you crying?"

"Of course, I'm not crying." She sniffed, turning her head.

"Then look at me." He hooked a finger beneath her chin and raised her face. Unshed tears filled her beautiful, green eyes. "I do believe you. I would have known was there someone else. I would have smelled him. And the only other man I sensed in your apartment was Sam." He raised a dark brow. "Unless—"

"Don't be ridiculous." She hammered his chest. "Sam is my best friend."

He drew her into his arms and rested his chin on her head. "I am not certain how this happened, and it did come as a bit of a surprise, but I am delighted. I suppose if we can accept that we were sent back two hundred years in time—" He looked into her lovely tear-stained face. "—I can believe a vampire fathered a child." He laughed shortly and dropped a small kiss on to her nose, using his thumbs to wipe away her tears. "Now where is the groom? He should have been here to take the horses. Wait here. I'll see if I can find him, then I'll get Mrs. Bosworth to fetch you a bowl of hot vegetable soup. You must be famished. I know I am." He moved down between the two rows of stalls, ten on each side, searching.

"Thomas! Get your laz—" His words died, as he found Thomas asleep on a pile of hay in the last stall. "Thomas." He nudged the boy with the toe of his boot, but he didn't move. A tight knot of apprehension formed in Vincent's stomach. "Thomas," he repeated quietly. "Wake up, boy." He crouched and rolled Thomas over. Gray eyes stared vacantly into Vincent's. On the side of his neck was a gaping bloody wound where she had ripped at his throat while sucking his life-force from his body.

Vincent dropped the boy and stepped back as the impact of what he was seeing registered. Epatha. *Epatha was here.*

"Alara!" He rose and sprinted down the aisle to where he'd left her. She was gone.

"Alara. Where are you?" He rushed to the door and relief flooded him as she turned back into the stable.

"I had to get some air; I was feeling—"

Vincent slapped a hand over her mouth. "Quiet. She's here."

Alara twisted out of his grip. "Who's here? What are you talking about?"

"Epatha. Thomas is dead."

Alara blinked. Her mouth opened and shut, and she released her breath in a rush. "How the hell did she get here?"

Vincent gripped her arms. Her words were strong, but her face was the color of ash. "My guess is Red-Cloud. How else?"

"She must have threatened his life. Oh, my God." Her hand went to her heart. "Charlie. He's in the house." She clutched his arm. "What if—"

"I am sure the boy is alive," he lied. He wasn't certain at all. In fact, he was terrified for Charlie's life. He lifted a small pitchfork from the stable wall and handed it to Alara. "Take this. Go to the last stall. Thomas's body is there. Sorry, but it is the only place I can think of where she might not pick up your scent."

He gave her a small push. "Move."

She took one step and stopped. "What are you going to do?"

"I have to find Charlie."

She gripped his arm. "Get the gun. It's under my bed in my handbag."

He nodded. "And if Epatha comes at you, point the pitchfork at her, heart level, and remember I love you."

She gave him a last look. "Me too, now go. I'm fine. I'm a cop, remember. I've faced villains before." She tried to smile but it came out more like a grimace.

He pressed a short hungry kiss onto her lips and stepped through the door.

It was raining.

****

He found the gun where Alara said it would be. Vincent pulled it from her handbag, checked the chamber—five bullets stared back from their housing. He stepped to the door and peered out along the dimly lit corridor. Nothing. The mansion was grave quiet.

He'd entered through the kitchen. The staff were dead, their throats torn and bloodied. The kitchen resembled a slaughterhouse. However, Vincent had witnessed Epatha take lives before. Somehow this seemed too much for one vampire, and it did not reek of her usual trademark. Epatha was a lot more fastidious in her kill, leaving only two small puncture marks, unless she'd been deprived for days, which seemed unlikely.

Vincent found poor Mrs. Bosworth face down at the top of the stairs. It appeared the old housekeeper had tried to run; a congealing pool of blood lay beneath her.

Epatha had not even fed. It was all about the kill.

With a silent curse, he crept down the hallway and stairs. He hadn't found Charlie. Hopefully, the boy had escaped. He reached the library and gingerly opened the door. Books littered the rug, where a small bookcase had overturned. Samuel was slumped across his accounts on the desk. A pistol lay on the patterned carpet just inside the door. Vincent picked it up and smelled the barrel. The gun had been fired but had been little use against one of Epatha's kind. The signs said it all. In frustration the old man had thrown the gun at her and tried to fight, but his struggle had been short lived. Samuel, being old, held little chance. He knew only too well Epatha's strength.

With a heavy heart, Vincent closed the door, but Charlie's voice, booming an expletive, had his chest pounding again. The boy was alive! He ran in the direction of the sound and stepped into the open parlor to see Charlie kissing young Mary. "Charlie, thank goodness—" He left the sentence hanging.

Charlie spun. Red stained his lips, and Mary's lifeless young body dropped heavily to the floor as he released her. "I tried to make her." The boy grinned, wiping the back of his hand across his mouth. "I guess I took too much."

Vincent shook his head. "Oh, Charlie. I am so sorry. I should not have left you. This is my fault."

"Don't be sad for me, Vincent." Charlie spread his arms. "This is what I wanted, remember? I begged Epatha to *make* me. It's what I always dreamed. Just wait, I will…"

Vincent shook his head. "You don't know what you are talking about."

"Of course, I know. I'm not a fool, though you

think I am." Charlie's tone chilled. "Everything is clearer, colors more bright. I can hear the blood running in your veins." Charlie's eyes glinted.

"Did you kill them?" Vincent asked.

"Not all of them, no. She stayed for a while." The boy shrugged and turned away to straighten a table that had been knocked over, probably in his struggle with Mary. "What's the fuss? They were only servants."

Vincent's jaw tightened. "Where is she now?"

Charlie's lips curved in a cruel smile. "She has a meeting to prepare for in London." The boy turned again to study a portrait of Vincent and his sister on the wall. "She really is lovely, your sister."

A frisson of fear raced through Vincent at the mention of Abigail, but he stemmed it. The boy was toying with him. He'd done so many times himself as a vampire before he'd taken his kill. Charlie was a quick learner, too quick.

"And Epatha left you here, why?" Vincent replied evenly, drawing Alara's gun from where he had tucked it into the back of his waistband, aiming it at Charlie's back.

"I had an obligation to fulfill. Where is our lovely Alara, by the way? She's pregnant, did she tell you? She told me this morning." He spun. "Congratulations—oh, I see. There's no need, really." Charlie spread his arms and moved toward Vincent. "I'm on your side. I just pretended so that I could help…"

He flew at Vincent, and Vincent pulled the trigger.

Charlie grunted and slumped, clutching his stomach. He glanced down at the red, rapidly staining his blue jacket, then up at Vincent, his eyes full of hurt.

"You shot me. I didn't think you would shoot me." He came unsteadily to his feet, and in a flash was gone.

"You darn fool, D'Amarno." Vincent knew he should have fired again, but he couldn't. It was Charlie, and he couldn't kill him, although he knew the boy would have drunk him dry without hesitation.

He ran for the door and took the hallway at a fast sprint, his only thought now for Alara. He broke into the courtyard to come face to face with her. The heavens had opened, and her hair and skirt were plastered to her body. She was the most beautiful vision he had ever seen.

She dropped the pitchfork and threw herself into his arms, and he dragged her up close and kissed her hard. "I told you to wait."

"I'm a sergeant detective. I give orders, not take them." She pulled away. "Did you find him?"

"Yes, I found him."

"Is he…"

"Not precisely, no. Epatha sired him."

Alara closed her eyes. "Poor Charlie. Why would she do it?"

"To kill us."

"And?" She glanced at the gun still in his hand.

"I wounded him." He rubbed at his temples. "I had a chance, but I could not kill him. Charlie was my friend."

Her arms came around his waist and she pressed her cheek to his heart. "I know. And I know it's hard, but it's not Charlie." She leaned back and looked into his eyes. "The Charlie you knew is dead. The creature who looks like Charlie is nothing like him. That creature is a cold-blooded killer and would feed on you without remorse."

He stroked her hair. "I above all should know that, but it makes it no easier." He held out the gun. "Take this. I have to bury the dead."

Alara stared at the mansion. "The servants?"

"No survivors, as far as I know."

"I'll help."

"No." He strode toward the house, and she followed. "You would not want to see what is in there."

"I'm a homicide detective. I've seen gruesome before."

"Not like this, you have not. Get into something warm. Take what you need from Abby's room, a woolen dress, a cloak, a fur muff, a bonnet, and some sturdy boots. I think her foot is about the same size as yours. As soon as the rain stops, we will start for London. My father took the carriage. We shall have to ride in the curricle. It travels faster but, unfortunately, there is no cover, so rug up and bring a couple of blankets. We'll stay in the village tonight and travel on to London in the morning. And…" He stopped and gripped her arm. "Mrs. Bosworth is at the top of the stairs."

"She's…"

"Yes."

"You sure you don't need help?" Alara caught his hand and squeezed it.

"I will call if I need you." He glanced away. "I am only grateful my father and sister were not here." He held her green eyes with his steady gaze. "You know we are going to have to carry out the plan alone now without Charlie?"

She nodded. "You worry too much. I didn't rise to

sergeant in one of the most crime riddled neighborhoods in Seattle without a few hard knocks. I'm tough. Trust me."

"Good." His tone hardened. "Because not only do our lives depend on it, but that of our baby's."

Chapter Thirteen

It was after dark when Sam slid from his new black Mustang across from Red-Cloud's shop. He patted the car roof. Alara would be proud of him. He had backed a winner today, paid off the rest of his mortgage, and bought his dream car. It was his last bet.

His arm still ached from the silver bullet the doctor had extracted, and he sported a limp from the bookcase that toppled onto his hip.

Shadows surrounded him and for an instant he thought he caught a movement in the darkness, and a hint of fear feathered down his spine. A black and white cat ran across the road beside him, and a small laugh escaped his lips. He steeled his resolve and walked on.

Epatha was gone. Red-Cloud had sent her back to the 1700s to find Vincent. As far as he knew no more vampires existed, or not in Seattle anyway, yet it was hard to rid himself of his apprehension.

He'd been a cop for over ten years, and nothing had chilled him like the look in Epatha's eyes just before she was about to have him for lunch. He would never forget those eyes, wine red and unflinching.

He rapped on the lead-light door and waited. Nothing. He knocked again and the door was dragged open immediately.

Red-Cloud ushered him in and closed the door behind him.

"Any luck?" Sam came straight to the point.

Red-Cloud remained silent and led him through the store and into the sitting room. He moved to the sideboard and sloshed a dash of whiskey into a glass and passed it to Sam. Then repeated the process and downed the whiskey in one swallow. He breathed out heavily. "I needed that, and no," he answered. "But I have not given up. I have contacted my father, and although he is old, he has agreed to travel here from Minnesota to help."

"What can he do that you can't?"

Red-Cloud poured another whiskey and sank into his customary armchair by the fire. "My father is skilled in the old ways. He was taught by my grandfather who was a great shaman. My sister has also agreed to combine her skills with ours. She is on her way from Ireland. Her plane arrives at six in the morning."

Sam frowned. "She lives in Ireland?"

"County Cork, to be precise. We were both raised by our mother. I left home at eighteen to live with my father, and to study psychiatry at Oxford." Red-Cloud smiled, showing his perfect white teeth. "My sister Colleen has gained a reputation among the people of our town of being a white witch. My mother used to say she had the gift."

"Used to?"

"My mother passed away three years ago. Brilliant woman. She was a heart specialist."

"Sorry."

"She lived to a good age and helped many. I am certain she has been rewarded in the afterlife." Red-Cloud downed his second whiskey, rose, and placed his glass on the mantel. He warmed his hands by the fire, cleared his throat, and faced Sam. "Now where were we? Ah, yes, bringing Vincent, Alara, and Charlie back home."

****

Alara stripped off her sodden, fur-lined cloak, gloves, and hat, and dropped them onto a rickety high-backed chair, the only chair in the room. She turned and stood with her back to the fire to warm her hands, and watched Vincent carry in their trunk. He set it down beside a four-poster bed, shrugged off his coat, and moved to join her. Taking her into his comfortable embrace, he touched his lips to her forehead.

"How are you feeling?" He tucked a knuckle beneath her chin and looked into her eyes. "The journey was not as comfortable as it should have been. The curricle needs new springs."

"Apart from being soaked to the bone, I'm fine." Alara forced a smile, feeling anything but fine. She was freezing. She gave a small sneeze, and a tremor ran down her arms and legs.

"I will have a bath brought up," said Vincent turning for the door, but Alara grabbed his arm.

"No need. Just hold me a little longer, so that I can soak up your heat."

He laughed softly, took her back into his arms, and gave her a gentle squeeze. "At least they lit the fire, and I have stayed here many times in my former past. The sheets are clean. It is one of the better inns on this road. Now, let us get you into bed." Tenderly, he turned her and proceeded to help her undress. She had to admit she was feeling tired. The trip to the tavern seemed to go on forever, and the icy wind and rain hadn't helped matters. If by some miracle she ever returned to her own time, she would never curse her little Firebird again. There was one thing she was grateful for, though—she hadn't experienced any morning sickness since yesterday morning. That was a good sign.

Alara stripped to her chemise and her own bra and panties and moved to the bed to slide in between the rough, cold sheets as Vincent pulled back the covers.

"Aren't you getting in?" she asked, watching him lift their trunk onto the bed.

He opened the lid. "I just want to double check that I have everything for tomorrow. I brought these clothes from the house. They are almost identical to the ones I wore the night I met Epatha."

"How do you remember?"

"I will never forget. That night lives in my nightmares. Even more so, since I returned home."

Alara reached out to pat his hand. "I'm sorry."

Vincent smiled down at her, then reached for a pair of fawn breeches, a blue velvet evening jacket, white linen shirt, and lacy cravat, and laid them in turn on the end of the bed.

"I wore a greatcoat very similar to the one I draped over the chair to dry. These are not an exact match, but it should not matter overly much. The original Epatha saw me only once, as far as I know, and that was at Covent Garden the same night she sired me. I doubt she took much interest in how I was dressed when she attempted her seduction later that evening." He ran a hand back through his short, black hair. "It is this that bothers me. It was much longer then. However, if we get to London early tomorrow, I can look up Thomas Harding, the wig maker my father uses. Hopefully, he will have a wig already made."

Vincent dropped the trunk onto the floor and unbuttoned his shirt, exposing his muscled chest, and her breath expelled in a rush. It never ceased to amaze her how the sight of this man, half naked or naked, did the most peculiar things to her stomach. He carried even more muscle now as a normal man than he had as a vampire. He stripped down, blew out the candle, and slid into bed beside her.

She sighed as his arms came around her and his male heat enveloped her in a warm, velvet cocoon. His hand cupped her breast, and finally his mouth sought hers, hot, almost savage, and she found in his kiss a desperation and passion that matched her own.

Now was all they had. Tomorrow, they faced an uncertain future and possibility of death.

****

This was a scene straight from Jack the Ripper, of that Alara was certain. Misty rain and no light except what exuded from sparsely placed lanterns hanging outside the doors of a few townhouses. She'd forgotten street lighting had not been invented until somewhere in the early eighteen hundreds.

She and Vincent had arrived in a hackney cab taken from the D'Armano residence. They had journeyed to the townhouse on the off chance that his sister and father were out and found they were in luck.

The London housekeeper informed them that Lord D'Armano and Miss Abigail were attending a ball. Vincent put their luggage in the library and with a frown from the housekeeper, Alara followed him upstairs to Abby's room. There she changed into warm dry clothes, and they made their final plans.

Vincent told Alara that if their plan to be rid of

Epatha and to save the other Vincent succeeded—they would never be able to return to Ashwood or this house again. He would take half his funds from the bank, not wishing to leave the other Vincent destitute, and in the morning, they would gain passage to India. There they would buy a plantation. He knew a man who would help them. It was a frightening new challenge and traveling on a ship at the end of the eighteenth century was not an experience Alara relished, but she had to stay positive. Vincent had sailed before, he had survived, and they would be together, she reasoned.

A dog barked at the end of the street and broke her from her revery. Shivering, she tucked her hands into her borrowed fur muff in an effort to regain some warmth in her cold fingers.

Vincent had given her a passion-filled kiss and left her on the corner with instructions as to how to recognize Lady Wilkes's townhouse. He'd also told her where to find him when she'd finished waylaying the other Vincent.

She peered through the darkness, barely able to make out the shape of several trees across the road. Vincent mentioned a park. She looked back at the houses she was passing and tried to distinguish the numbers. Finally, she found the number she needed a few steps ahead. A bright lantern hung beside the number one hundred and seventeen. She had no idea what she was going to say to the other Vincent.

She knew she should have planned, but nothing came to mind. Vincent had told her he'd been a bit of a charmer, so perhaps she could ask for directions and flirt a little. What the heck. It had worked for Epatha. Why not her?

****

Vincent checked his fob watch. Again, it read eleven thirty p.m. He was certain the meeting with Epatha had occurred around eleven fifteen, because he'd checked his watch when he'd stepped from Charlotte's townhouse that night. He had gained only a few paces around the corner before Epatha had emerged from the shadows.

He waited for over twenty minutes and still she did not show. Somehow, he had missed her. He went to push his hand through his hair then remembered his wig and cursed. There was only one thing to do and that was to go on to the place Epatha had attacked him. He hesitated, thinking of Alara, but knew he had no choice. Alara had the gun. Hopefully she would not hesitate to use it should she run into trouble.

He broke into a sprint, frantic now to stop Epatha, cursing at the darkness and uneven cobblestones that hindered his path. His breath came harsh in his ears, and the cold evening air chilled his lungs. He stopped to gain his bearings, trying to think. They had turned left here and crossed the road. Again, he ran, knowing he must hurry. If Charlie had told Epatha of their plans, she might already be there with his other self. He couldn't let that happen. Only God knew what would occur if Epatha achieved her terrifying agenda. And what of the original Epatha? Where was she?

****

Alara drew to a halt at the bottom of the steps leading up to Charlotte's townhouse, the green-eyed-cat-of-jealousy eating at her stomach.

She clenched her hands, her nails digging into her palms as she waited. Vincent told her that he'd made love to Charlotte on this night, that the woman had been his mistress.

Alara knew she shouldn't be jealous of something that occurred over two centuries ago, but she couldn't help herself. Vincent was Vincent in any shape and form. He was her man, and she loved him. It hurt her that he should be in that house with another woman.

She was almost tempted to knock on the door, but he wouldn't know who she was. She thought she was reconciled to the fact, but now she wasn't certain. However, she would do her job. Then she would go on to the lane and meet *her* Vincent, knowing he loved her in return.

Hopefully, he'd have dealt with the real Epatha by then.

Vincent knew the vampiress's weakness was somehow tied up with the red stone in the necklace she wore. The woman had hinted at it on several occasions. He also carried an antique silver dagger he'd taken from the weapon collection at Ashwood. If he was unable to gain the necklace, he would use the dagger.

Alara was brought from her thoughts by the opening and closing of the townhouse door. For a heart stopping moment she thought it was the man she sought, but as he stepped into the light, she recognized him as Charlie.

She was about to smile and speak when she remembered he'd become Epatha's plaything. Instantly, she was flooded with sadness, only for it to be replaced by a hint of fear, as she caught the gleam in his eyes as he glanced down and saw her.

Her fingers tightened on the gun tucked securely within her muff and she straightened.

Charlie wiped the back of his hand across his mouth and took a step down the stairs, but stopped as he recognized her. She saw him hesitate and frown, then he smiled, which was even more chilling. He appeared so much like the Charlie she had come to know and like, with his spiked brown hair, innocent pale-blue eyes, and infectious grin. It made her heart hurt.

"Alara, great to see you. What are you doing here?" He took a pace toward her.

"Stop right there, Charlie. I know what you are. Vincent informed me how you attacked him, what Epatha did to you."

The boy stilled, and the smile dropped from his face. "You're too late. He's gone." He looked at the wristwatch he'd brought from the future. "About twenty-five minutes ago."

"How did you manage that?"

"I told the butler that Lord Wilkes's meeting had finished early and that I was a messenger from her husband. Lady Charlotte was to ready herself. They would be attending a ball. Vincent's double left the house soon afterward to be waylaid by...well you know the rest of the story."

"And the occupants of this house?"

He grinned. "I think you know the answer to that one."

Alara's heart hardened. "I'm sorry, Charlie." She knew she'd have to kill him, yet even as she thought it her mind rebelled. She couldn't kill Charlie.

"Sorry for what? I wanted to be like this. Did Vincent tell you how many times I begged him to sire me? It's great. Everything is so clear, smells, though the sewers and garbage in this town stink. My hearing, if I stop and listen, I can even hear the water running in the drain two blocks away."

His eyes glistened in the pale moonlight as the clouds chose that moment to roll aside.

"Join me, Alara. Epatha is already being a pain. It's do this, do that, go here, go there. Drink his blood, drink hers. Let me make you like me. We could go anywhere, do anything. Be rich as kings and queens." He spread his arms.

"Murder innocent people and drink blood for eternity and never see Vincent again. I think not," she retorted in cold sarcasm, and all animation fled from Charlie's face.

"I'm sorry you said that, Alara. I really did like you." Two large teeth appeared from his top gums and his eyes transformed to a glittering wine red. He gave a guttural hiss and flew down the steps, but she'd already pulled the gun and fired. He tumbled down the last five steps and rolled over ready to leap, and Alara fired again, emptying the last three rounds into his heart. She'd always been an excellent shot, and tonight was no exception. Her bullets had found their mark. He slumped to his knees, and in that last instant, reached out his hand, and Alara could have sworn it was the real Charlie that was trying to smile through. Or was it just her wishful imagination?

He fell face down and she knelt, rolled him over, and closed his large, blue eyes. His canines had retracted, and it was not like the movies at all. The vampire did not burst into flames, or turn to dust; it seemed to revert to the person it had been before.

She was certain this was Charlie she cradled in her

arms, or she wanted to think so. The pain cut deep as she stroked his pale cheek. His face, ice cold.

She hadn't known him long, but what she had known, she had liked—his quick wit, his cheeky grin, his ability to always say something funny even at the most inappropriate times. "Goodbye, Charlie, it was a pleasure to know you."

She laid him back to the ground and stood, wiping the tears from her eyes. "I am certain you are in a better place now, my friend. May we meet in another lifetime." She wondered when a vampire died if their soul lived again. Then she pushed the thought aside as fanciful.

She had to think of Vincent. What had crossed his mind when Epatha hadn't been waiting? Had he raced on to the lane where the attack had occurred? If so, he could be in mortal danger, for he would come face to face with his double, and who could say what disruption it could cause to the cosmos? As far as they knew, Vincent was safe as long as he didn't encounter his other self, but what would happen if he did?

****

Vincent stopped. His lungs craved air, and his sweat-soaked shirt stuck to his back. The rain had ceased, and the moon broke through the clouds, but the wind was still a bitter sting against his heated flesh.

He hesitated at the alley alongside the dilapidated building, The Old Chancery Inn. A mental picture flashed in his mind of the attack in the alley all those years ago. It seemed like yesterday, the pain so fresh. A shiver prickled his skull then ran the length of his body. Sweat beaded his forehead. Although it terrified him to the bone to enter this dark place again, he knew he had no choice if the other Vincent was already in there, Epatha at his throat.

The weight of the silver dagger in his greatcoat pocket lent him a small amount of comfort. And Epatha did not know he was coming, that was some advantage. Her necklace would not give him away, as he had not yet been sired, or he was sure he would feel different.

Drawing Alara's small flashlight from his other pocket, he stepped into the alley. He did not switch on the light as he would only use it if completely necessary.

A startled cry in the darkness, a woman's voice and the sound of a scuffle had him forgetting that thought.

She had him.

He switched on the flashlight and ran, but what he found about twenty paces away had his footsteps freezing. He remembered this exact same moment. It was him, but not him. He was an observer of his own life. And if he did not act quickly that life would soon be over!

He shone the flashlight directly into Epatha's eyes. She cried out and reared back, and her victim sank to his knees.

"Get up, you fool! Run!" Vincent shouted, but still stunned by the impact of his attack, the other Vincent turned to face him.

Vincent dropped to his knees clutching his head, as a bright light exploded before his eyes. A roaring like the ocean filled his ears, his vision cleared, and he heard Epatha's voice.

"Who are you?" Her eyes widened, as she stared from one Vincent to the other, her fangs retracting into her gums, and her eyes reverting to turquoise.

Vincent floated on a sea of pain, ever so slowly forward, incapable of stopping. He knew his other self could feel it too, by the look of horror on the man's face. He managed to maintain his grip on the flashlight, and it shone on his double. The other Vincent's face ashen in its beam.

A dreadful cry broke into the darkness, wrenched from the depths of both their guts, and a fearful ringing like a thousand church bells assailed Vincent's ears. Scalding needles attacked his limbs, and he was moving, faster now like in a dream, but not. He saw the shock in the other Vincent's eyes as their bodies slammed and merged—disorientation, blackness, and then a bright light. He opened his eyes, and they were as one, and all of his memories came rushing back, of now, of yesterday, of both minds, of his vampire days, of his trip to the Americas, of…Alara.

Then she had him! Somewhere in all the haze, in all the memories he had forgotten his true reason for being here. Epatha!

Her breath came in a foul-smelling hiss, and fear washed over him in an ice-cold shiver. Her arms encased him in bands like steel. He struggled, attempting to break free, but his efforts brought a smile to her lips. He'd been here, he'd done this before, and once again she held him imprisoned.

"Too late, my pet. You are mine."

He brought up his knee, aimed at her stomach, but she twisted and slammed him into the wall. He should have remembered. The breath knocked from his lungs. He sank to his knees only to glance up as moonlight caught the glisten of her pointed teeth emerging from her top gums.

He pulled the knife and waited.

Cunning showed in her eyes, and her laugh broke free. "Do you think you can defeat me with that piddling skewer?" She flew at him.

Knocked off kilter he stumbled, stabbing wildly in the dark. A cry tore from her lips and the knife flew from his hand, to clatter noisily onto the cobblestones.

Sweat slicked his back, and his heart slapped into his ribs. She stepped back for a moment, contemplating the wound in her shoulder, then agony struck in terrific speed as she lifted him and sunk her teeth into his neck.

Pain tore through his innards, and he brought his fists down into her head, but her hold was a vise, of which he could not break free. The struggle was exhausting and the pain radiating from his neck died to a dull ache.

He sensed the blood draining from his body, lethargy setting in. He was dying, powerless to stop Epatha for a second time.

Cold, then warmth. She had won.

His soul was lifting. He floated, dreamlike, weightless, and hovered in a meadow of mauve-blue heather, watching himself as a babe with his mother. The scene changed. He was a boy of twelve, kneeling at her bedside. A baby cried and he held his mother's hand as her soul slipped from her body. Years raced by in quick succession—his first horse, his sister's fifth birthday, the joining of his first men's club, his first woman and…Alara…and his baby. He couldn't die, he had to fight, but even as the thought registered, he settled into an ocean of darkness with a faint beacon of light in the distance.

Then he heard it, Epatha's voice.

"Get away from him, you cow! He's mine!"

He struggled to open his eyes. The moonlight brighter now. The flashlight still glowed, and in that glow, he spotted Epatha. The one he knew. The one who had sired him.

In an instant, she bounded at the Epatha kneeling over him. But she was ready for her. The Epatha who attacked him leapt and grasped her twin's arms. A blinding flash of light filled the alley, and in that moment, they merged, just as he and his double had merged. Vincent saw the confusion on Epatha's face, the disorientation and horror in her eyes, then he sank into…deep darkness.

****

Alara prayed she would be in time. She had gotten lost at least twice and stopped now to gain her bearings. A half-broken sign hung sideways several feet above her, pronouncing the building, The Last Chancery. The doors and windows were boarded black, yet its white brick sides stood out in stark contrast against the grimness of the night.

This is it, the building Vincent described.

She peered into the alley and spied a faint glow in the distance. Fear, unlike any she had ever known, filled her. This was where it had taken place. This was where Epatha had made Vincent a vampire. Had she succeeded in doing so again? What if she was too late?

A woman's scream from within the alley propelled her into the darkness. She ran now as if her life depended on it, or Vincent's did. She approached the light, realizing it was her small flashlight, and watched the two Epathas merge as one. There was a cry and a bright flash of light, and the remaining Epatha sagged to her knees, clutching her stomach, as if in dreadful pain.

Alara didn't falter. She spied Vincent lying prone beside Epatha, and her rage ignited. She charged at the vampiress and wrenched the necklace from her neck. She dropped the stone to the ground and brought her heel down hard, once, twice, hearing it crunch beneath her boot. "Take that," she spat in satisfaction.

Epatha stared wide-eyed at Alara, and her hands went to her head. "What are you doing?" she screamed. A touch of horror laced her words. She sprang to her feet and raised her hands backing away.

Then an unholy scream erupted from deep within her throat. In the light of the moon, her face changed, at first slowly, then in rapid succession. Alara's stomach knotted and with sick revulsion she watched Epatha's silky black hair fade to gray, the flesh of her face age and fall to flab, her body wither and cripple with age. Her clothes fell to rags around her feet, her flesh peeled back, and her skeleton burst forth and exploded to dust. The breeze caught it, and with a quick gust lightly sprinkled it across the alley.

Alara stood stunned, unable to move, unable to believe what had happened. Her gaze drifted to Vincent and a sob broke from her throat. She raced to his side and cradled him in her arms, feeling for a pulse on his bloodied neck. It was there, but weak. He'd lost so much blood. Too much.

She looked at the pile of dust lying on the alley floor and knew if she could take Epatha's life all over again she would gladly do it. She held Vincent to her chest and leaned to kiss his cold lips.

Tears trickled down her cheeks, and impatiently

she brushed them aside, swallowing the lump in her throat. He was dying, and there was no way she could stop it. She had loved only twice in her life, and she would lose them both in the same manner. If she'd been in her own time…maybe a blood transfusion, but there were no hospitals she knew of here. Any doctor would look at her stupidly, even if it were possible to find one.

She was alone in the 1700s. How would she survive without Vincent—even if she wanted to? She gulped, as another sob broke from her throat, and she put her head down, holding her man close to her heart, and wept.

Something broke through her subconscious and she struggled for composure. How long had she cradled Vincent in her arms, giving free reign to her tears? She didn't know, but as she opened her eyes, she realized they were encased in white light. Sparkles filled her eyes, her mouth tasted of earth, then a tearing sensation, like being drawn along at an awful speed. She couldn't open her eyes…blackness engulfed her, her thoughts grew garbled…and…

****

Alara opened her eyes. She hadn't even known they were shut. She was sitting on the bearskin rug in Red-Cloud's living room, still cradling Vincent in her arms. Long narrow sticks lay scattered haphazardly about her—the remnants of Red-Cloud's magical tepee. Looking down at her were four pairs of eyes.

Sam rushed to her side and never had she been so delighted to see his rugged, handsome face. Red-Cloud was there, dressed in his white jeans and fringed shirt.

There were two strangers. A kind-faced woman with black and silver hair, wearing a full-length dress and ebony fringed shawl. It was the fourth occupant of the room that grabbed her attention. He could have stepped out of a John Wayne movie.

Ancient and shirtless, his face streaked in red, blue, and yellow, on his head he wore a hat made of buffalo horns. She gasped and clutched Vincent tighter as the man dropped down beside her and reached for Vincent's wrist to feel for his pulse.

"Don't be afraid," he said, looking kindly into her eyes. "I'm a doctor." His voice was nothing like she expected. Warm, cultured, professional, it held a wealth of comfort. He turned to Sam. "Call an ambulance, quickly. He needs a blood transfusion." He glanced up at the woman. "Marion, hot water, and anything I can use as a bandage, Stan." She hadn't known Red-Cloud's name. "Blankets, we have to get him warm." Then he gently pried Vincent from Alara's bear-like grip and laid him on the rug as Marion and Red-Cloud rushed back into the room to cover him with blankets and administer to his wound.

Sam hung up his cellphone and pushed it into his pocket as the doctor brought Alara to her feet and released her into Sam's arms. She went there willingly, clutching to him as if he were her lifeline, and if she let him go, she would be sucked back into the unknown.

She held close to Sam's chest for several long minutes, then finally gaining some measure of control over her shaking body, looked around as Red-Cloud touched her shoulder.

"The boy, Charlie. He is not with you?"

"No." She thought she could be strong, but as she spoke the words, she felt a dam burst inside her. "Epatha turned him." Tears filled her eyes and choked her voice. She swallowed. "I had to shoot him." She turned back into Sam's shoulder, and hot tears slid down her cheeks.

His arms came around her and she wept aloud. She was home, yes, and Vincent had been saved from becoming a vampire, but at what cost?

Epilogue

15 months later

Alara sat beneath a tall, flowing willow on the grassy Sydney foreshore. A bright sun shone overhead, filtering down through the branches of the trees, throwing glitter across an azure bay and reflecting off the Harbor Bridge.

She turned at a child's giggle. Her heart swelled with love as she watched Vincent playing *toss the baby in the air* with their six-month-old son.

They had named the baby after Charlie. He had Vincent's midnight hair, wide green eyes, and an infectious grin.

She'd worried for a while after their return from the past that she would not be pregnant—that with all the confusion of time, something had happened to take her baby from her. An ultrasound had proved her child still existed and they'd both been delighted.

As for her and Vincent, they were married in a quiet ceremony with only Sam, Red-Cloud, Marion, and Red-Cloud's father in attendance. After Vincent's blood transfusion and long recovery, Sam had advised them to disappear. Vincent was still wanted in relation to the McManus killing. Sam had told everyone she'd taken ill and had gone on a long vacation to recover. He had also collected Jesse from her apartment after

Alara's disappearance and was looking after her. She had already planned to have her little Siamese transported to Australia.

Alara had spent her childhood in Sydney. She'd been happy here with her parents and brother and liked to think they were looking down on her now that she was home.

Vincent set the baby on the woolen rug, and his arm snagged her waist to pull her close. "Happy?" he asked, touching his lips to hers.

"Ecstatic. You?"

He nodded. "Of all the places I and Epatha traveled, we never came to Australia. This is truly a wonderful land." He raised his face to the sun, then looked down into her eyes. "A place of sunshine and love."

"Only you could make it so." She cupped his cheek, and he smiled and took her lips in a passionate kiss that promised all and everything for the rest of their days, and all their lives to come.

Thank you for purchasing
this publication of The Wild Rose Press, Inc.

For questions or more information
contact us at
info@thewildrosepress.com.

The Wild Rose Press, Inc.
www.thewildrosepress.com